# S is for Serial

D. K. Greene

Copyright © 2015 D. K. Greene
All rights reserved.
ISBN: 1517482992
ISBN-13: 978-1517482992

Amy—

So glad you made it to the release party. Love you guys so much.

P.S. Don't use any of the tips in this book, no matter how tempting it is.

4

# A Note From The Author

I am fascinated by serial murderers. I assume since you are turning the pages of this book that you have interest in them, too. You may read crime novels and indulge in some light reading about the heaviest serial murderers in history. There is something a little off about you, but that's O.K. because there is a *lot* off about me.

As I worked on this bit of fiction, I wrote with the assumption that you have a lingering interest in people who hunt other people. I also took on the notion that you love the unsavory details of those stories. Keeping these assumptions in mind, I hope you will be delighted to discover that many of the locations mentioned within this book are real. I took many field trips so that I could stand with my characters on the ground where their misdeeds take place.

Although many of the locations in this book are real, this is a work of fiction. The characters are plucked from my imagination and don't exist in real life. None of the events actually occurred. The whole thing is a farce, which is a fact that I hope keeps my family warm at night.

## Many Thanks

This book would not be what it is today without the advice, support and guidance of many people. First, I must thank Keith who is the best editor and partner in crime that I could ever hope for.

Next, I must thank the early readers. Susan, who got a very early copy and hasn't yet suggested that I be exorcized. Corie and Clay for their professional notes. Elise, Jeanne and Sarah for helping to tweak things.

I am so appreciative of Jacobsen's Books & More in Hillsboro, Oregon. If you happen to stop in, please tell Tina that she is beautiful and her efforts to support local authors are greatly appreciated.

Thanks must go out to all of the people who I have ignored during the making of this book. If your phone call wasn't answered or your e-mail was not returned, your irritation was an investment in getting this book made.

8

# Prologue

The air is thick in the Deputy Warden's office. Ollie looks out through the rattling panes of the room's only window and watches as orange and red leaves fan across the glass on what is probably a crisp fall wind. It has been so long since he's felt a breeze on his skin that he struggles to remember what it feels like.

"Another Bible study group." Deputy Warden Hazel pulls off his glasses and shakes his head. The barrel-chested man rubs the lenses on his shirt before he returns them to the tip of his nose. "What in the hell is wrong with the group that meets on Tuesday?"

Ollie looks down at his shoes. They lie perfectly even side by side below the edge of his chair. The lace on his right shoe flops across the tip and the knot has begun to loosen. He concentrates on worrying that it might catch on something when he stands up at the end of this meeting. He imagines himself falling.

9

Hitting his head on the desk's sharp corner. If it tore the skin deep enough to bleed, Ollie can't help but wonder what pattern the blood might make as it pools.

Once the worry lines are embedded in the creases of his face, Ollie looks up. "I've been asked to not participate in that group."

The Deputy Warden doesn't look sympathetic. "Give me the names of the inmates. I'll make sure they know that you're allowed in, same as them."

"I understand my being there is hard for them. I don't want to encroach on their ability to share in the Lord together. It isn't just me. Sanders and Winter want to study the Bible, too. Let's just say that the three of us don't inspire much faith in others."

Deputy Warden Hazel smirks. "I suppose not. That doesn't mean that my staff should have to create a whole new program. There's no payoff for the prison."

Ollie nods, hiding his eagerness behind the worry of his shoelace. "It could help. It might distract the others from their anger. Give them a positive focus while they wait out their time. It could help keep them so busy praying that they won't think to cause problems."

"And what do you get out of it?" The Deputy Warden leans forward. Thin strands of blonde hair catch the light of the window behind him. As sunlight glows around Deputy Warden Hazel's head, he takes on the visage of a very conservative angel.

"I've come to terms with my past being wrong. I wish I could go back out there and make a difference in the world, but I know that will never happen." Ollie lets a solemn tear trail from his wet eyes. "But I still have a calling. A duty to be my best. If I can help just one other person to find the strength to make a change, then none of this will be in vain."

Deputy Warden Hazel shakes his head. "I can't just let a serial murderer start a prayer group."

Ollie slumps against the hard plastic of the

chair behind him. The light has passed from behind the Warden's head. The magic of the moment broken. "Is there anything I can do?"

"What is it that all you Christians say? Actions speak louder than words?" The Deputy Warden points at Ollie's file splayed out across his desk. "Get your ass out there and make a difference. Prove to me you are ready to stop holding onto all those secrets. Then we'll talk about what to do with your Bible study."

## Therapy

I have been Peter James Wilson longer than anyone expected. I've had enough time to get a college degree, land a decent job, and keep a girlfriend long enough to celebrate an anniversary. I finally have a normal life. Almost.

If I was really normal, I wouldn't be seated in a therapy session with a woman who doesn't know my real name. She's going to spend weeks trying to solve the puzzle of my constant anxiety and fear of abandonment. I already know the answer, but I won't tell her that. Maybe she'll figure it out one day.

If anyone knew that I was in therapy, without being able to talk to my therapist about why I needed to see her, they might think that it was a waste of time. And maybe it is, but in some weird way it makes me feel better to talk about the banality of normal, average problems.

"Peter?" Doctor Richards uncrosses her legs and leans forward. As she scoots against the leather chair her knee-length skirt raises up her thigh an inch. She doesn't notice, and I do my best to not be distracted by it.

"Yes?" I realize my gaze has lingered a moment too long when her hand tugs the fabric back

13

down to the top of her knee. I snap my focus to her eyes.

"We're about halfway through your session time, and you haven't said much. Is there anything you'd like to talk about today?"

"I'm sorry, Doctor. I've never done this before. I don't really know what to say." I shrug my shoulders and slouch into my chair. It's a lie, of course. This is my sixth attempt at therapy. I don't have any medical history as Peter though, so I pretend it's new to me. It makes it easier to explain away all the things that I can't say.

"Please, call me Jeanne." She smiles a practiced smile, one designed to break down barriers and open a subject up. Police interviewers do the same thing when they talk to kids. "Let's start with why you decided to come and see me."

"OK, Jeanne." I look down at the hands folded in my lap. One of my thumbs twitches involuntarily. "Well, I guess I just wanted someone to talk to."

She nods. "Do you have many friends?"

"No."

"What about family?" Jeanne reaches for a pad of paper on the table beside her and scribbles a note.

"My mom died when I was twelve." I try to

appear sad, the way someone who lost a parent is supposed to. The funny thing is, with all the lies that I will tell Jeanne in our sessions, this story is actually true. But after two decades of life without Mom, I'm just not that tore up about her any more.

Jeanne nods again, but her face takes on the same practiced sadness that I'm expressing. "And your father?"

"We don't talk." I fidget in my chair, unsure of whether to say more or not. The words wrestle on my tongue for a minute and then I blurt out, "He's incarcerated."

Jeanne takes the information in stride. It must be strange to spend your days talking to fucked up people. I imagine a person in Jeanne's profession eventually reaches a point where nothing is shocking any more. "It must be lonely without many friends or family to talk to."

I'm nodding before I realize it. It is lonely being the only one who knows who you are. "I do have my girlfriend."

"What's her name?" Jeanne's hand becomes still, poised over the paper.

"Elsie."

Jeanne smiles. She recognizes Elsie as a way to

15

get me to talk. I can tell that she is looking forward to the rest of the session passing by without us just staring at each other in silence like the awkward strangers we are. "And how did you meet?"

"We met at a cemetery." I look toward her pad as it fills up with scribbles and wonder how much more truth I want to tell her.

"Did someone you know die?" Jeanne turns her mouth down in another sympathetic frown.

"An acquaintance. I didn't really know him, but my dad did." I stop short of telling Jeanne that while Elsie knew his name, I only knew the man as Victim 32. "He was Elsie's dad. It was kind of funny, we both decided to visit his grave on the same day. It wasn't even a holiday or anything."

Jeanne smiles with me. "It's interesting how things work out sometimes, isn't it?"

"Yeah. Although sometimes I wonder if meeting me was really the best thing for her." I don't like to think about how Elsie and I met. Most of the time I can push it out of my mind. That's probably why Elsie finds a relationship with me to be so easy though. We both lost our fathers when we were young and had to learn to navigate the world without them.

"Do you not feel worthy of Elsie?" Jeanne's

head tilts curiously. She reaches a hand across the small space between us and places it on my knee. I can feel the warmth of her palm through my jeans. Her fingers rest around my kneecap and squeeze slightly when I try to shift away from them. "Many people feel unworthy of love when they lose their parents as children. That doesn't make it true."

I feel the tears start to well up behind my eyes. I hate this part of therapy – the part that's real. I try to push the tears back but it's a losing battle. Suddenly Jeanne's hand disappears from my knee and is replaced with a small cardboard box. I pull a stiff tissue out and hide my eyes in it for a second. When I pull it away I see Jeanne's sympathetic facade, but know that deep down she is proud of being able to strike a nerve. I'm reminded that therapy is nothing more than a manipulation of character. Her job is to unbury people's secrets, and for twenty years my job has been to keep them.

"Love doesn't exist." I choke on the words a little when they come out.

Jeanne scribbles another note. "How long have you and Elsie been together?"

"A year."

"A year is a long time to be with someone if

17

you don't believe in love." Jeanne doesn't look at me as she speaks. She's distracted by writing her notes and it makes me feel uneasy. I suddenly feel the need for her full attention. I wring my hands together to keep from grabbing her face to force her to look at me.

"It seems to work out well enough just liking her," I offer.

"Does Elsie know that you don't love her?" Jeanne looks back at me and the tension melts away.

"I don't know."

As Jeanne leans forward, her skirt rises along the edge of the chair again. This time I vow not to stare at the smoky nylon tights that cling to her thighs under her hem. "Have you ever told Elsie that you love her?"

"Yes, of course." I lean forward in my chair, too. Jeanne smells nice, the scent of plump strawberries and bowls of warm buttermilk waft off her skin.

"And you don't feel bad about lying to her about your feelings?" Jeanne's eyelashes flutter as she frowns at me.

"I do, sometimes." I think about Elsie and realize I've been waiting for Jeanne to kiss me. The idea of cheating on Elsie makes my stomach turn and I lean back in my seat. I feel the stomach acid rise in my throat and I try to force it down.

"Are you OK?" Jeanne reaches for the tissues again and pushes the box further up my lap.

I swallow hard and take a few deep breaths. "Yeah. I think so."

"What happened? You looked very ill just then."

I think for a moment, trying to find an appropriate response. "I was just thinking about what you said about lying to Elsie. About how she'd feel if she found out the truth." I nod and am relieved when Jeanne copies my movements.

"Maybe you care more about Elsie than you realize." Jeanne touches my knee again and the warmth of her hand makes my skin tingle beneath the thin denim.

"Maybe I do."

## Elsie

Elsie is waiting for me when I get to my apartment. She's parked in the space out front, settled into the backseat of her car. Her laptop is open and she's surrounded by books. I tap on the window and the music pours out at me as she rolls it down.

"Hi!" Elsie shouts over the wailing radio. She picks up a remote from the pile to her right and shuts it off before I have to ask. "I was wondering when you'd show up."

"Homework?" I gesture to the mess in her backseat and she nods back at me.

"Morin has us doing research on singular organisms." She snaps her laptop shut and somehow manages to exit the backseat without spilling her books out onto the pavement. "Did you know that there is a forest in Utah made up of one tree? It shoots roots out and sprouts more trees, but they're all a part of one root system."

Elsie pecks me on the cheek and walks toward my apartment. Without looking back at her car, she pushes a button on the fob that makes the window roll up and locks the doors. I follow her.

"I didn't know that. Sounds interesting. How

long have you been out here?" I struggle to get my keys out of my pocket. By the time I make it to the door Elsie is watching me, impatient.

"About an hour. I need to use your bathroom."

I nod as the key turns in the lock. Elsie pushes by me before the door is open and rushes down the hall. I try to think if I've left any weird old man paraphernalia out on the bathroom counter, but she's shut herself in there before I have a chance to remember the nose-hair clipper sitting by the sink. I shrug my new jacket off my shoulders and am hanging it up in the closet when she comes bursting back out of the bathroom. Elsie explodes into and out of things everywhere she goes. I don't think anyone ever taught her how to tiptoe.

Elsie grabs my face and looks up my nose. "You missed a hair."

I feel my skin flush in embarrassment when she laughs at me. Then I realize that it's meant to be a joke so I pretend to laugh with her. "Sorry, I didn't mean to leave that thing out."

"Don't apologize," she chastises me for the hundredth time. "It's your apartment. You can keep whatever crap in here you want."

Elsie hugs me, but reaches behind me with one

21

hand. She pulls the jacket that I was just wearing back off the hanger, then races across the apartment with it. "Except this. This thing is awful! What kind of fabric is this, anyway? Tweed? Shit, could you possibly wear anything more boring?"

"The lady at the store said it looked nice. Dignified." I sit down on the sofa. I know Elsie won't give the jacket back so there's no use in chasing after her.

"This woman you speak of. Was she the same woman who sold you the jacket?"

I nod, and a tidal wave of Elsie's laughter crashes against me.

"You're too trusting, Peter." I watch as the brown and gray jacket falls down into the garbage can at the edge of my kitchen counter. Elsie reaches for the day-old pot of coffee and pours it out over the jacket.

I push my anger at Elsie's destruction of the jacket aside because I know there is no use in yelling. She will just laugh at my outburst and fly out of the apartment for a few days until her transgression blows over. I don't want to be alone so instead of fighting with her, I lean back on the couch and sigh. "At least she didn't charge me full price."

"Thank God." Elsie laughs. She lets her foot

slide off the pedal on the can and the lid snaps shut.

"So, did you save enough money on that jacket to take me out to dinner tonight?"

"Of course."

"Good. Let's go somewhere expensive."

## Contact

Elsie is out with a study group and I've never brought anyone else to my apartment so I rise from the couch with hesitancy when there is a knock on the door. I pause in the center of the living room in silence, waiting for the visitors to announce themselves or leave. I jump when the rapping resumes.

"Just a minute." I look for something to hold onto in case the person slamming their fist against my door is a robber, or worse, some religious fanatic here to tell me about the "good news". I settle on the big dusty Bible that lies on the bookshelf near the door. Whether I need to hit the offender with it or start proclaiming I already have enough faith to smite unwanted visitors, it will have to do.

I look through the peephole and find the funhouse image of a man standing too close to the door. The glass warps his forehead into a kid's swimming pool. His arms and legs dangle from his chin like waves of crate-paper on a badly constructed piñata. I hold my Bible close and open the door the few inches allowed by the fastened chain.

"Henry?" The normal looking man leans into the open crack. "Henry Roberts?"

I freeze. I try to sort out who this man is and how he has access to my real name. He is just an average middle-aged man in a dark black suit. He holds a binder in his hands and his hairline is on the retreat. "Sorry, man. No one by that name here."

"Oh, of course." The suited intruder looks down into the binder and flips through a few pages. "It's Peter now, right?"

I take a step back from the door. "Who are you?"

The man gives a warm smile. He wipes his thin hairline with his sleeve. "Oh, I guess you wouldn't remember me. I don't think I've seen you since you were – what – fifteen? You went by Charles then, or was is Chuck? I can never keep track of these things."

"I don't know a Charles." I move to close the door.

"I'm Inspector Douglas. I helped out on your dad's..."

I cut him off. "I called you Dougy."

"That's right! Inspector Dougy. Man, that got under my skin after a while." He gives a slightly irritated chuckle.

I stare through the crack at him. Dougy has gained a considerable amount of weight in the last

25

seventeen years. His hair is not only thinner than when I saw him last, but it's also a decidedly lighter gray than I remember. He'd worn a biker jacket and beard then. Now he's clean shaven and wears a suit that looks too big for him. I wonder if he is losing weight, or if he is in the habit of buying clothes one size too big "just in case".

Dougy breaks my thoughts. "Do you mind if I come in?"

"Yes."

He unbuttons his jacket and stands up a little straighter. His shoulders broaden and he takes a bullish stance. "Well, will you let me in anyway?"

I push the door closed just enough to slide the chain off then open it wide so that Dougy can push past. He stops in the middle of my living-slash-dining room and takes it all in. "Henry, you've got a nice place, here."

"Thanks." I close the door but leave it unlocked in case either of us have to make a hasty exit. "Call me Peter. What are you doing here?"

"Mind if I sit?" Dougy doesn't wait for me to answer. He sits down square in the middle of the couch and puts his binder on the coffee table. He leans into the cushions, arms across the back of the couch and

26

crosses his legs. "Say, Henry. Do you mind if I have a glass of water? It's been a long day."

I shrug and take a few steps into the next room to retrieve a glass and fill it in the sink. Dougy starts talking as soon as the faucet turns on, and I can't make out what he says. I'm just around the thin white wall that houses every cabinet that my six hundred square foot apartment has. I yell around the corner, "Just one second."

When I return to the living room I find Dougy in the same position but now his binder is open and papers are spread neatly on the coffee table. I hand him the glass of water without looking at the photos. I've seen the victim's photos dozens of times. They have been displayed on the news, in the papers, and during the years of interviews following my dad's arrest they peppered the table of every meeting.

"I spoke to Ollie this week." Dougy takes a sip of the water, then sets it down on top of a stack of papers. He picks up one of the photos and offers it to me as if I might want to look at.

I concentrate at looking out the window. "Oh? I thought he was giving everyone the silent treatment."

Dougy lets out another low, nervous chuckle. He still proffers the photo. "He had been. But all of a

27

sudden this week he's decided he wanted to have a conversation. You know how Ollie is. When he wants something, it's hard to say no."

"Harder for some than others, I guess." I rub a clammy hand across the back of my sweating neck.

"Yeah, I guess." Dougy struggles up from the couch then takes a few steps to close the gap between us. He puts a firm hand on my shoulder, then pushes the picture into my face with his other hand. "He says he wants to talk about Carol. Show us where she is."

I study the top right corner of the picture. It's a faded blue, the color of a background drenched with the flash of thousands of driver's license photos. "So?"

Dougy clears his throat, shifting uneasily on his feet. There is a tenseness about him that makes me glad that the door is unlocked. Maybe he will make a run for it. I glance at him sideways and realize that if he does, he will probably pass out in the breezeway.

"He says he'll only talk to you."

# Visitation

"Henry." Ollie starts to stand up, but the chain attached to his wrists catches on the chair and he stops half way.

"Hi, Dad." I sit down opposite of him. He looks exactly the same as I remember from my childhood. Being locked up away from the sun has preserved him. He smiles the same smile that he used to give me when I got an A on my report card. I start to smile back, but when I rest my hands on the cold steel table between us I'm reminded of where we are.

"It's good to see you. You're all grown up." There's a proud gleam in Dad's eye, and he moves to touch my hand. The gesture might have moved me when I was younger.

I've spent a lifetime trying to forget we are related. The thought of his skin touching mine makes me feel ill. I pull my hands back from the uncomfortable gesture and put them in my lap. "Yup. I'm thirty-two, now."

"Where does the time go?"

Seeing my dad beaming across an industrial table at me, clad in an orange jumpsuit, wrists and ankles chained together at my request, has officially become an even more awkward family reunion than I had imagined it could be. I glance toward the nearest guard and wonder if he can hear us over the chatter of the other people.

"So, Dougy says you want to talk to me?"

Dad laughs, and I'm filled with the warmth of his happiness. "You still call him that? He hates it, you know."

"I didn't ask him to show up at my front door. I'll call him whatever I want."

Dad nods, pleased at my defiance. "I'm glad you came. It really is good to see you."

This time I smile back at him. I hate to admit it, but it is nice to see him, too.

"I decided that it's time to let Carol go." Dad's face drops as if he's a farmer putting down his favorite dog. "I got a letter from her daughter. She wants her new baby to have a place to visit her grandma. I think that's a good enough reason to let go."

This time I'm the one that reaches forward. I touch his hand gently, and he responds by pulling my hands into a fierce grip. "I'm glad you're ready for this one, Dad. Maybe after Carol we can find a few more."

"Maybe." Tears form in Dad's eyes and I know that his 'maybe' really means 'probably not'.

"So, I'm here. What's next? Are you going to draw me a map or something?"

Dad cracks a smile. "No. I don't think I can picture it well enough right now. It's going to take a couple visits to jog my memory."

I sigh. I should have known it wouldn't be that easy. "OK, Dad. What do you want to talk about?"

"You, mostly." Dad beams again. "Tell me about yourself."

If Dad won't give up information I don't know how long the guards are going to let us visit. In the interest of time, I dive right in. I tell him about Elsie, my apartment high in the hills of Northwest Portland, and my job as an engineer at Ronix. He's particularly interested in my work and we talk for a while about program errors and office politics.

"Your boss sounds like a real dick."

I nod. There's nothing to do but agree. "I can't take much time off to come see you, Dad. We're going to have to work to find Carol on the weekends."

"Forests in the Northwest are so beautiful in the fall." Dad closes his eyes in a moment of nostalgia. He breathes in deep as if he's pretending to smell the wet leaves. Then I remember what kind of monster he is and wonder if he discards the smell of leaves and

31

imagines the smell the decomposing bodies instead.

"So Carol's in the woods?"

Dad only opens one eye, but the disapproving glance makes its mark. "I never said she was in the woods, Hen. I was just making a casual observation."

"Right." I nod. "We're done for today, then."

Dad's face falls but he mutters that he understands. A guard is beside us before I've pushed my chair back and then I know for certain that our conversation wasn't private. Conversations between the other inmates and their families stop when a second guard joins Dad to help him shuffle with his chains back toward his cell. Dougy waits for me in the hallway and he pats me on the back as I walk by. "She's in the woods. Good work, Henry. Good work."

"It's Peter now." I brush his hand off my shoulder and head to the exit.

# Reconnection

The clock in Jeanne's office ticks louder than any other clock I've ever heard. I decide that if I'm still seeing her during the holidays I'm going to buy her a digital wall clock. She's wearing slacks today. I hope I haven't turned her off of skirts. They suit her.

"So, what's happened since I saw you last?" Jeanne braids her fingers around her pen and rests it on her chest.

"My dad contacted me."

Jeanne tries to be a portrait of professionalism, but I can see her perk up. A normal client wouldn't notice the way her eyebrows twitch and her mouth purses in anticipation the way I do. She leans over her pad of paper and checks her notes to make sure she remembers correctly before she comments, "Didn't you say that he has been in jail for an extended period of time?"

"He's incarcerated, yes."

"How did he contact you?" Jeanne bats her eyes at me, and I know that she is hanging on my every word.

"He wrote me a letter."

"Did you happen to bring it with you?" Jeanne

inches toward me. She anticipates me handing over a letter that drips with emotional trauma. I hate to disappoint her but I hadn't thought to make a letter up to bring with me.

"No. But I can tell you what it says."

Disappointment is masked by a calm smile as she leans back in her chair. "Sure, if you'd like."

"He says that he misses me, and that he wants to see me." Jeanne scribbles on her pad. I keep going, enjoying her excitement. "He says that he knows he was wrong. He hopes I'll forgive him and that we can be a family again someday. You know, when he gets out."

Jeanne glances up at me. "Will he be released soon?"

"Oh, yes," I enthuse. "He should be getting out sometime in the next few weeks, I think."

"How did that letter make you feel when you read it?" Jeanne's eyes dance at me.

"I don't know." I sit and think for a while. "On the one hand, I guess it's nice to have him paying attention to me. On the other hand, I don't really want to get involved in his shit."

Jeanne nods and I know that she understands what I'm saying. Trying to fix a jailbird parent is a tough proposition for a man with problems of his own. I smile at her and she smiles back. I enjoy our conversations so much that I wish I could tell her this outside of her office. I imagine we are talking over dinner. I can almost see the candlelight flicker off her cheeks.

"What does Elsie think you should do?"

I stop fantasizing about red wine shimmering off of Jeanne's lips. "I haven't told her."

Jeanne writes something down and underlines it. I want to know what she wrote but I'm sure she'll never show me. It probably says something akin to *doesn't trust girlfriend*. I cringe because if that's what she wrote, she's right.

"I don't talk to her about my dad," I sputter.

"Because your fathers knew each other do you think that it will stir up bad memories for her?"

I nod so deep that my chin touches my chest. To say that the topic of my father might wound her would be an understatement. "She doesn't know much about my dad, other than that he's gone."

Jeanne looks surprised. "Oh? Have you never told her that your fathers were friends?"

"No. I don't think it would be good for her to find out how they knew each other." I can't sit down

35

any more. I look at the clock and am relieved that it says it's five minutes to noon. "Damn. Looks like our time is about up, Jeanne."

Jeanne follows my gaze and frowns. I can tell that she feels things are just getting good. "I suppose it is. Well, make sure to stop at the front desk to book for next week. I look forward to continuing our conversation."

We lock eyes and when Jeanne smiles I decide that I was wrong about not believing in love.

# Relationships

"I stopped by your office to surprise you with lunch today." Elsie speaks around a mouth full of noodles. She sits cross legged on the floor, hunched over the coffee table for what she calls a "true Asiatic eating experience".

"I must have just missed you." I talk at the back of her head from where I sit at the dining room table. It used to be awkward but this disjointed eating arrangement has become our norm. I see her throw an annoyed glance over her shoulder. I try to convince her by adding, "I decided to go out for lunch today."

"You don't eat lunch, Peter."

"I had an appointment. Is that OK?" I hate the way she dances around things. She never just comes out and says what she wants. Just tells me everything she knows about me and then tries to catch me in a lie.

"What kind of appointment? You obviously didn't get a haircut, and you're still wearing the same crap you always do." She turns and looks at me squarely. "And I know you're not sick, so don't pretend to cough or feign a fever."

"I don't 'feign' things, Elsie. The last time I said I had a fever, I actually had a fever." I pick up my half-

37

finished dinner and carry it into the kitchen. It's a relief to be out of sight, away from her accusing stare. I stand at the sink and listen for a moment, waiting for her to get up and follow me into the kitchen for a fight. Instead, her chopsticks clink against the side of her bowl and I know she's not mad enough to make the effort.

I take my time emptying my bowl in the garbage and rinsing it out before I put it in the dishwasher. If I take long enough, maybe she'll realize I don't want to talk about it. Hell, if I can stretch the act of washing this one dish out for a half hour maybe she'll finish her food and leave. I'd rather deal with the annoyance of her dirty chopsticks spreading sticky sauce across the coffee table than have a fight with her.

I look down at the now spotless dish and realize I'm being ridiculous. I set the bowl and fork in the dishwasher and muster the strength to go back to the living room. When I round the corner she is typing away at her laptop and doesn't even notice me. I move over to her and bend down to rub her shoulders.

"Jesus!" Elsie shrieks and jumps under my touch. She slaps the laptop lid closed and spins around on me. "How many times do I have to tell you not to sneak up on me like that? Fuck, Peter, clear your throat

38

when you're about to approach or something."

"Sorry." I shrug and move so that the coffee table is between us. I stare at her, unsure of what to do to make her feel more at ease. She glares at me and I sink down into the couch. The way she looks at me makes me wish I could disappear.

"It's fine." She spits the sentence out at me with venom. Then, as if she realizes what a bitch she's being, she smoothes her hair and smiles at me. "It startled me, is all. You're just so quiet. You know?"

"Maybe I should tie some bells to my socks." I smile at my own joke even though she obviously doesn't get it. I point at my feet and wiggle my toes. "For the noise."

"You're so weird." Elsie rolls her eyes before she gives me her smile one more time.

"Do you love me?"

Elsie's smile fades and her eyebrows squish together on her forehead. "What?"

"I've just been wondering if you love me." I do my best to not look like a lost puppy but judging from the pout of Elsie's lip I am probably failing.

"Honey, there's lots to love about you. You're kind, have a good job, and always bring me Phò noodles when I ask for them." Elsie beams at me.

"You love me because I order Vietnamese noodles?"

"Absolutely." She crawls around the coffee table and pats my foot reassuringly. "Well, that and you don't mind me doing homework all the damn time."

"I suppose happy relationships have been built on less." I look out the window and think about how worried Jeanne seemed to be about my not loving Elsie. I decide to try harder. "Hey, do you want to spend the night tonight?"

"Here?" Elsie bursts into laughter. "Peter, you have a twin bed."

"The couch pulls out," I offer.

"Aww, honey." Elsie pushes out her lower lip again, but this time she forces it to tremble. "I'm really sorry. I've got a big test tomorrow. Plus, my parents expect me to come home for dinner."

I point to the empty bowl on the coffee table. "We just had dinner."

Elsie stares at the bowl with me. Then she whips her head around with an apologetic frown. "Well, yeah, babe. But they eat dinner late. And they've been planning this dinner party for weeks."

"Can I come with you?"

She sucks air in through her teeth, making a

40

sound that makes me squirm. It's something she does whenever she's nervous. "Oh, Petey, I wish you could. But, you know. Dinner reservations. I can't add a party guest this late in the evening."

"I understand." I slouch a little lower into the cushions.

"Why are you asking all this?" Elsie's tone is accusatory and it makes me want to shrivel up and die.

"I don't know. It's just that we've been together for a year now. It seems like it's time to make things a little more serious." I look to her for agreement. "Isn't it?"

Elsie shakes her head and laughs. "Oh, man. You had me going for a minute. First with your disappearance at lunch, and then wanting me to stay the night and meet my parents..."

"I don't understand. Isn't that what you want? To be more, I don't know. Together?"

"Babe, I am just fine with things the way they are. We don't need to rush into anything, or take what we have to the next level." She pats my foot again. "I'm getting everything I need out of this relationship. Aren't you?"

I nod although I'm not sure. I need to be close to someone. Although Elsie shares part of her life with me, she is always so buried in the chaos of the life of a grad student that sometimes I feel I hardly know her.

"Good. Let's not push anything, OK?"

"OK," I agree. "But if you ever want more, just tell me."

"I promise," she smiles. For once, I believe her.

# Push

"I asked Elsie to stay the night with me last week." I hope that Jeanne sees this as personal growth. Actually, I hope it makes her jealous.

"How did that go?" Jeanne presses her pen into the bottom of her chin as she leans forward with interest.

"It went well. She wants me to meet her parents." I smile.

Jeanne raises her left eyebrow and she pushes back through a couple of pages of notes. "I thought you said that her father was deceased? That you met – yes, that you met at her father's grave site."

I hadn't even thought of that when Elsie mentioned going to see her parents for dinner. "She has a step-father. He's been a part of the family so long that she says he's like a real dad."

Jeanne nods, satisfied with my answer even though I have no idea what I'm talking about. It would make sense though. If her mom remarried when she was little, wouldn't she think of her mom's husband as a second father? I nod to myself. Absolutely.

"Have you met many of Elsie's friends?" Jeanne's pen moves from her chin to the corner of her

43

lips.

"No." Jeanne scribbles a note and I try to think of why I've not met anyone Elsie is acquainted with. "We aren't really into the same things. She's in college, and I'm set in my job at Ronix."

Jeanne looks concerned. "Do you ever think it's odd that you and Elsie aren't closer?"

I ponder the question a minute. "I don't think I know how to be close to anyone, Jeanne."

"Why not?"

The answers bounce around in my brain and I try not to spit them out. *Because even my foster parents didn't know who I was. Because this is my fourth identity since being put into witness protection. Because doesn't everyone just walk around pretending to be someone they're not?*

"I'm not sure."

"Do you think it might have to do with a fear that people will find out that your father is incarcerated?" Jeanne frantically scribbles a note, convinced that she's on to something.

"What do you mean?" I watch the way she bites her lip. Her lip gloss shines below the short row of teeth pressing down on it.

"Sometimes when a person is embarrassed

about their parents, they have a tendency to pull away from other people. It is as if they carry the shame of their parentage around with them. A proverbial 'monkey on their back', as it were."

"I'd never thought of that before, Jeanne. I suppose I do feel that way."

Jeanne reaches across the sitting area and clasps my hand in hers. My fingers stay flaccid, but she grips me tightly. "You need to understand that you are not your father, Peter. Whatever he did to get arrested was his doing, and his doing alone. You were only a little boy and had no control over the situation."

"I'm the one who called the police," I blurt. I pull my hand away from Jeanne and use it to cover my mouth in shock at my own admission.

Jeanne's eyes grow a little wider. "You did?"

"She-she was bleeding. Everywhere, blood everywhere. I wanted to save her. She was all that I had. I loved her so much." I stammer the words from behind my hand and they come out muffled but it's obvious that Jeanne understands. Tears stream down my cheeks and although I want them to stop, I can't keep them from falling.

"Oh my God, Peter. What happened?"

I look down at my feet and can almost see the

45

blood pooling around them. My mother's eyes look up at me, pleading with me to help her. I'm on the phone with 9-1-1, and I try to remember my address so that the ambulance can come and save her. When I mix up the house number my mom just smiles at me. She exhales a deep breath that comes out as, "I love you, Hen." And then she's gone.

I manage to stop the tears. I mop my cheeks with a tissue and look up to see Jeanne's anguished face begging me to tell her more. Jeanne is right. I was just a kid. It wasn't my fault. "My mom asked my dad to give something up, and he stabbed her to death in our kitchen."

"Jesus," Jeanne whispers.

"No shit." I nod.

"What was it she wanted him to stop doing?"

I've got to come up with an answer and think of all the things that my dad did when I was a kid. I shuffle through the lists of things that normal parents would do. He didn't keep many vices. Just the one. "He did taxidermy as a hobby. It took up a lot of his time. She wanted him to stop."

"That's an odd hobby." Jeanne's concerned eyes shift in thought. "He must have been very passionate about it to have killed your mother."

46

My head bobs again in agreement. "I haven't spoken to him in years. Now, all of a sudden, my dad wants to talk to me again."

Jeanne sits silently. I can see the wheels turn in her head as she tries to decide what advice to give. None of the options are that great. I know, because I've been over them a million times. I could tell my dad to go fuck himself. But then I'd have to carry the guilt of all of the families waiting to find their loved ones. Or, I could suck it up and see how it goes.

"Do you think your dad loved your mother?"

"More than anything. Well, at least as much as the taxidermy." I laugh, but Jeanne doesn't bite. I can tell she doesn't want me to joke. "He didn't fight the police when they came. He cried a lot and promised me that he loved me and that he didn't mean it."

"Do you think that your father committed a crime of passion?"

The laugh that comes out is involuntary. Jeanne's serious face reminds me to stuff the humor. I straighten up as best I can. "Yes. At least one."

I think you should talk to him." Jeanne sets her jaw. "People do change, Peter. If he truly loved your mother then all these years behind bars without your support have been punishment enough. If the court

47

system thinks that your dad has paid his debt to society then I think you should give him a chance."

I really thought Jeanne would advise me to let my dad shrivel up and die in his own filth so her advice catches me off guard. "You think so?"

"I do." She smiles at me and pushes a loose hair back behind her ear. "Besides, at this point, what do you have to lose?"

## Killing Flies

I'm back in the visitation room with my dad. We make awkward small talk for a minute and then finally I can't stand the tension any more. "I need to know where Carol is, Dad."

"Right this second?" He looks genuinely confused. "I thought we could get to know one another a little more first."

"You know everything that you need to know. I've grown up. I became a man. I have a job and pay taxes. I've got a view that looks over the backside of Providence Hospital and I drive a Honda. Ta-da!" I wave my hands in the air.

Dad leans forward and smiles, "Hen, what is your most notable achievement?"

"What?"

"When people see you walking down the halls at Ronix, what do they whisper about you?"

My face scrunches. "I don't know, Dad. Maybe, 'there goes that guy who didn't fuck up the big product push this week.' Or maybe they just gasp and fan themselves because they know all of my 0's and 1's are in the right order."

"Exactly." Dad's fist pounds the table. "You're

49

going through the motions, Son, but none of those people knows just how special you really are."

"Special? I don't know what you're talking about, Dad."

"Hen, you are the son of a great man. And that makes you a great man." The wrist that he lifts from the table is thin and frail beneath the weight of the handcuff. But the finger he points at me is strong. Decisive.

I nod to the orange jumpsuit. "A great man, huh? You sure don't look it."

Anger flashes behind his eyes and I know I've hit a nerve. "Only great men have to be kept locked up so that the world cannot see them. It's the mindless drivel that gets put out on display."

"Whatever." I pull a piece of paper from the corner of the table and push it toward him. Then I take the soft, floppy "please don't stab me" prison pen and hand it to him, too. "Just show me where Carol is, Dad."

"Show me that you are good enough to know where she is, Son." His voice drips with disdain.

"Fine." I hold up the fingers on my right hand and start counting them off. "I've got a great life. I've got a great job. I've got a great girlfriend. I've never been in trouble with the law, despite the fact that my dad murders people faster than God can create them. And five – well, I guess five is that I pay my goddamn rent on time."

"But what have you really done?" Dad holds three fingers out and counts them off, too. "You live alone in a tiny apartment with stark white walls and secondhand furniture. You're dating some average little girl who only loves you because she misses her daddy. You work in a tiny cubicle. Shit, Sherlock, that's only three completely stupid things. You're no better off than me, Hen. The only difference is that while people shiver when they hear my name, there is nothing remarkable about you. You're no better than all those stupid people clocking in and clocking out every damn day of their lives, begging for someone to kill them to make it all stop."

"You don't have to kill someone to be great, Dad." I wish I could punch him.

"Uh huh. How about you just start small then. Think you could kill that fly?" My dad lifts his cuffed hands as high as they will reach and gestures to a fly pattering against the glass of the window beside us.

"Fine." I get up from the table and reach out for the tiny fly. I don't know what the point of this is, but I've swatted a hundred flies in my lifetime. I close my hands around the bug and bring it down to the table. Killing a bug is stupid. Simple. It's a pest and its death shouldn't arouse any emotion.

But I do feel something. I've got an ache in my chest because I know that I don't have to kill it. Its wings flutter against my skin and I feel its tiny feet scramble across my palm. It is alive and in a moment it will be gone forever. I think about just getting up and letting the fly go outside but as I look into my father's eyes I feel helpless to stop. I close my own eyes and clap my hands together.

When I open them, I see the fly lying limp in the palm of my hand. Its wings bent, its legs askew, and its entrails dripping across my hand. I wipe it off on my jeans and turn toward my dad. "There, are you happy?"

My father shakes his head in disappointment and suddenly I am transported back. I'm just a little kid and he's pointing to the shattered glass of my mother's favorite vase strewn across the dining room floor. I half expect him to pull a belt from his waist to begin my punishment.

"I'm not happy. And neither are you. You kill a fly the same way you do everything. Fast, efficient, and without any purpose."

52

I look down at the bug guts smeared across my pant leg. "I did what you asked me to do. The fly is as dead as it can get."

"Sure, it's dead. But you killed it the same way every other schmuck would kill it. Where's your interest? Your creativity?" My father leans back in his chair and sighs. "If you have it in your mind to kill something, you might as well give it some finesse. Answer some questions. Find some pleasure in it."

"You want me to take pleasure in killing a fly?"

"My God, Son, yes! If you are going to steal a life, you both should take the time to get something out of it. Now that poor fly will never know what it's like to live a life without wings. It'll never know how it would survive with only four legs instead of six. You'll never discover how many of its guts you could squish out while keeping the damn thing alive. What you did was cold blooded, and you know it. There was no benefit to either of you, and that's what makes it murder."

"And exactly what did you teach your victims, Dad?"

"Son, I gave those people faith."

Every one of my dad's victims had no god before they entered his truck. Over the years of his

53

trials, Dad swore that they had faith by the time they came out of it, no matter how many pieces they were in at the time. It didn't matter to him if you were Christian, Muslim, or in a cult or praying for aliens to abduct you. Hell, as long as you wrote a sincere letter to Santa every year, you were probably safe. But if you didn't have some faith, well, Dad was on a mission to show you the error of your ways.

"What if they lied to you? What if they just told you what you wanted to hear so that you'd let them go?"

My dad looks down at his hands. His thumbs twiddle with a practiced swivel that keeps the chains binding him silent and unmoving. "Hen, do you remember Ted?"

"You know I do."

What I hadn't told Jeanne, and what most of the journalists and true-crime authors fail to print about my dad was that he didn't just do taxidermy as a hobby. It was a practiced art. While most families had pool tables and media centers in their basements, we had a taxidermy workshop. Dad could have done the gig full time, but he said that he enjoyed it too much to make it into a job. Nonetheless, his work could still be found on display in most of the museums in the Northwest. Bears,

54

cougars and coyotes are sprinkled around the country's most well loved exhibits with his name tagged under the fur.

Ted was Dad's most prized work of taxidermy. He was a big guy. He stood above 6 feet tall, and when he was alive he would have weighed well over 250 pounds. How Dad moved him from our basement to the cab of his rig without anyone taking notice is still a mystery. Dad kept him under a false floor in the semi, and anyone who ever lied to him would get a ride under the floor with Ted until they decided it was time to tell the truth.

The thing about Ted, as Dad tells the story, was that when he was alive he was a notorious liar. Once preserved from hair to toenail, Ted couldn't lie any more. I only met Ted once. I was six and in a fit of boyish hyperactivity had colored on the living room wall with Mom's lipstick. When confronted with the evidence I did what any intelligent boy would do. I blamed the dog.

I didn't have to ride in the truck with Ted because Dad recognized that would probably be too much for a six year old to handle. But I did have to take a long look at him lying in there while Dad told me his story. Dad said that if I ever lied again, then that is

55

what would happen to me.

Dad clears his throat, breaking my memory. "Hen, do you think there is a person alive who would lie to me after they got to know Ted?"

I shake my head. "No sir, I suppose not."

"That's how I know all those people had faith in the end."

"Whatever, Dad." I rise from the table and walk toward the door. I take solace in knowing that this is something that Dad probably won't do again unless I agree to help. If I refuse to walk the woods with him to uncover Carol, then he'll sit in this cinder-block hell until he dies. I put my hand on the doorknob and turn back to him before I go. I raise my voice enough that he can hear me over the low chatter of a dozen other conversations. "Thanks for the talk. I hope you rot in your cell, all alone just like Ted."

I open the door and take a step outside. Before the door closes he calls after me.

"Hey, Hen. Just so you know – that guy they called Victim 32 didn't have any damn kids. He had a couple of ferrets that he loved to bits, but no wife or toddler running around that dump he called an apartment."

I shake my head and let the door fall closed

56

behind me.

# Field Trip

Dougy stands on the corner to sneak a cigarette before we head into the Tillamook Forest. I'm sure he's one of those guys who blames the smell of cigarette smoke on younger officers when he gets home to keep his wife off his back. I don't know how a man whose whole career has centered around murder can be so spineless when it comes to women.

I check the lock twice before I walk to the car with him. I try to stand out of the way of his smoky exhale but the wind shifts and blows it into my face. "I don't know how I let you talk me into this shit, Dougy."

"It's for the families," he reminds me. "Besides, one day when this is all through people will see you as a hero."

I don't know if the job of digging up bodies my dad has hidden will ever be through. I do know that I feel something reminiscent of closure when I drive up to see Mom's headstone though. I want to give Carol's family that feeling. "Let's go."

We get in Dougy's unmarked car and head out highway 26 towards the coast. The clouds above us are ominous and the radio announces a threat of thunder storms. The search crew had tried to reschedule, but it took so much work for Dougy to get approval for Dad to leave the prison that he put his foot down.

We pull off the highway near Brown's Camp and work our way down a jackknifed trail just wide enough for the car's mirrors to clear the shrubs. We come around a turn near a clearing and I see a nondescript panel van and two cop cars parked in a row. Dougy parks at an angle, cutting off the narrow entrance to the clearing.

"Is everyone ready?" Dougy calls out as we approach the vehicles. No one answers.

I'm filled with dread. What if Dad figured out how to get away? I imagine that we're going to come around the side of the parked vehicles to find officers' bodies strewn throughout the forest. I'm nauseous as I picture their entrails hung in the low branches of trees like Christmas ornaments.

I hold my breath as we round the bumper of the last car. No one is dead. Instead the marshals and officers are huddled in a semi-circle, laughing. Everyone holds a lit cigarette, even my dad. They almost have the appearance of a bunch of buddies ready to go hunting, aside from the flash of police lights and FCI SHERIDAN printed in bold prison letters across Dad's back. I exhale with relief.

"Shit, boys. This isn't a social gathering. Let's get to it." Dougy barks at the officers and they all duck in embarrassment.

Dad looks over at us. "Ah, Inspector Douglas. It's been a long time."

Dougy looks as if he might punch Dad in the throat. "It has."

"I was thinking." Dad gazes off into the woods. "Maybe you'll let me and my boy walk off a little ways so we can talk? I think it will help jog my memory a bit to feel like I'm on an afternoon hike."

Dougy pulls me close and whispers, "You don't have to do anything you don't want to, Peter. If you don't want to be alone with him, we will sure understand that."

"It's OK. I don't mind."

Dougy frowns. He almost looks fatherly for a second. "If he says or does anything that makes you feel uncomfortable you just raise your hand. You raise that hand, and we'll come and get you."

I nod, then shuffle through the dense layer of leaves toward my dad. "Shall we?"

Dad looks as giddy as a kid with a bucket full of candy. He'd probably skip down the trail ahead of me if it weren't for the cuffs still around his ankles. I

60

check to make sure he's got enough movement to step over fallen branches. Satisfied that we'll be able to make it down the trail together, I start to walk into the woods.

"Isn't this nice?" Dad didn't peep a word until we were out of earshot of the officers, but now that he's sure they can't hear us he starts to talk. "We used to go on hikes all the time when you were little. Remember? Man, nothing beat all those summers camping out under the stars together. S'mores that filled our stomachs and scary stories that filled our heads."

I give a curt nod. Camping out in the woods with Dad would have been some of my favorite childhood memories, had I ever cared to think back on them. "I don't think about being a kid much."

Dad shakes his head. "All that media attention, I know. It really put a negative spin on things for you."

I look at him in disbelief. "You killed people, Dad. *That* is what put a negative spin on things."

"Aw, son. What I did in my spare time wouldn't have had any impact on our family had the damn reporters stayed out of it. I took good care of you and your mother. I hope you know that."

"Until you killed her." I intend the words to cut like a knife, and am satisfied when he winces.

61

"Yes. Well, I wish to God that I could take that back. Life without her is -" Dad's breath catches in his throat. "Hard."

"I'm sure that Carol's kids feel the same way." I look off over the sea of brambles to the side of the trail and wonder which tree has spent decades protecting her.

"I don't think anyone feels alive until they know what it is to have someone they love die."

I look at Dad sideways. "Do you seriously believe the shit that falls out of your mouth?"

"Yes, Hen. I do." Dad glares at me seriously. "I didn't truly understand the preciousness of my work until I lost your mother. All those years I thought I was just saving the souls of the people who came to me looking for truth. But in reality, I spread a thread of hope out across all of the people who ever knew them."

"You mean, all the people who hoped they were still alive."

"Of course."

"But then they found out that they were dead. Mutilated. Sewn up with all the glitz and glamour of side-show freaks and dumped in the woods. That kind of unravels the thread of hope, Dad."

He walks off a few more paces, his focus on

nothing but the path in front of him. He knows exactly where Carol is but he won't to look in any direction that might give away her location until he is ready. He turns around to look at me. "All you have to do is show someone that a thread of hope exists, and they will hold onto that thread for the rest of their lives. No matter what else comes up along the way."

I'm about to yell at him for being such a jacked up psychopath when the thunder cracks overhead. The rain starts to fall in golf ball sized globes through the canopy and both Dad and I trot back up the trail to the search team. We can hardly hear one another talk over the roar of water cascading through the forest, so we point to the vehicles. Dougy nods and sloshes through the quickly rising mud to his car. I meet him there and we duck inside. We're both drenched and the downpour slaps against the windshield so heavy that we can't see even when he turns the wipers on.

"Did he give anything up?" Dougy presses the gas lightly and somehow we're able to back up onto the road without getting stuck. I look back toward the van as it climbs the ascent behind us, the glare of its headlights the only thing I can make out through the rain.

"Only that he thinks that he's a stellar parent."

Dougy's hard laugh competes with the sound of the rain. "Father of the year, I'm sure."

# Work

"Can I talk to you for a minute, Charles?" I lean against the gray wall of my boss's cubicle. His back is to me, and the only acknowledgment that he gives that he heard me is his index finger held up in the air. I wait, glancing up at the clock every so often to watch the minutes go by. Finally, I clear my throat again.

"Oh, sorry. I didn't realize you were still here." Charles turns in his chair and I see what was so important. He has several sets of curved scissors and some fancy paper strewn across the back side of his desk. An open container of glue drips onto the Formica and I try not to smile as he shoves pictures of his dog under the pile.

"I am. I need to talk to you. Do you mind if we talk in a conference room?"

Charles looks at the clock. "I have a meeting in twelve minutes. You'll have me for ten."

We walk across the vast cubicle filled space until we find a side room not in use. Charles flips the sign on the door to "In session" and then plops down at the head of the table. I choose a seat on the corner beside him and we stare at each other.

65

"Eight minutes." Charles taps his wrist where a watch would be.

"Sure. So, I have some stuff going on and I think that it would be easier for me to take care of if I took some time off." I fidget in my chair.

"What kind of stuff, Pete?"

"Well, family things mostly."

Charles looks at a clock hung on a support pole outside of the conference room. "You've never mentioned much about your family before. What's up?"

"My father is – ill."

"Huh. Is it fatal?" Charles looks impatient.

"Well, it might be. I mean, it has been for some people." I evade his gaze by looking down at my sleeve.

"Take it up with HR. If you can furnish proof that he's gonna kick it, well then there's nothing I can do to stop you from leaving. But you've got to cross those I's and dot those T's. You know what I mean?"

I nod. I know exactly what Charles means. He means that he doesn't give two shits about what happens to me. He's got a quota to meet.

Charles slaps me on the shoulder. "Good meeting. Let me know how it all shakes out."

I stay seated, watching as the door closes

behind Charles. I lean over to the speakerphone on the table. I pull a piece of paper out of my pocket and dial the number printed on it.

"Human Resources, Susan speaking. How may I help?"

"Hi, Susan. This is Peter Wilson. Badge number UB-13854. I just found out that my dad is dying, and I need to file for a leave of absence."

"Oh, Mr. Wilson. I am so sorry to hear that. Let me pull up your file. There you are. I'm e-mailing you the approval form right now. Please hand it in to your supervisor before you leave today. You will receive three days paid, and can take up to an additional ten days unpaid. How long do you think you'll need?"

"Susan, my dad has stage four cancer. The doctors have given him six months. Isn't there some kind of extended leave I can take? I really want to be there for him." I push out some false tears and hope that the sound of my crying makes it through the line to her.

"Oh. Yes, we do have an extended family leave option. Combined with your accrued vacation time it looks like you can take up to 16 weeks. I'm sorry, but anything past your vacation time will be unpaid. Do you think you can make it that long

67

financially?"

"I'll have to find a way, Susan."

## Understand Me

"I've been thinking." I look at Dad as he tilts his head to the right of the path. The entire search party notices the gesture and abandons their search of the bushes to the left of us.

"You seem to do that a lot." I keep pace with him as he wanders down the narrow dirt trail.

"I'm afraid there's not much else for me to do these days. But, I digress. I think that if you had ever killed someone, whether for love, or hate, or boredom, then maybe we wouldn't be at such odds all the time."

He says this as if he's talking about me picking up a new hobby in shuffleboard or chess. I shake my head. "I won't murder someone just so that we can fucking connect, Dad."

He stops in his tracks and takes a long look at me. "Why not?"

"I don't know; because people are *people*? Jobs, families, lives to live?"

"Not everyone has a life worth living. There's a lady in D block who killed seventeen people in hospice that didn't have anyone to visit them. You could think of it less as murder, and more as putting someone out of their misery." He shrugs off my frown. "Fine, then.

69

Let nature take its course."

We stand in silence a moment. Me, staring at this man who used to be my loving father. He, deep in thought working out the problem of me not being able to walk out and choose someone to squeeze the life out of.

"Not every murder happens from a guy choosing his victims. You could always figure out a way to let them choose you."

I groan and look up at the trees. I wish one would fall over suddenly and knock us both down, dead. "Come on, Dad."

"I'm serious. Let's say you held some kind of contest. It could be totally random. Hell, you could even just put a prize in a Cracker Jack box that explodes when it comes in to contact with moisture or something."

"Shit, Dad! Little kids try to win prizes out of Cracker Jack boxes. As much as I'm not a murderer, I'm certainly not a pedo-murderer."

"Hey, I understand. You want a victim to have a little life experience before he dies. Or she." Dad shrugs as he makes a concentrated effort to not be sexist. "Although there's always orphans and kids from crack houses. They've got plenty of life experience."

We walk a little further down the trail. Dad's train of thought is so absurd that I don't even know how to respond.

"Hasn't anyone ever pissed you off so much that you just want to..." he holds his hands out in front of him and mimes choking an invisible person to death. Dougy is near the end of the path we're on and notices the gesture. He raises an eyebrow at me. I shrug and motion that I'm OK.

"Not really."

"Not even me?" Dad looks at me with interest. "I killed your mother, then got hauled off to prison. I left you to be raised by strangers. Not only did I stick you in foster care, but I also made you grow up around the discovery of dozens of murders and caused you to get involved with the clean-up."

I sit down on a stump and gaze up at my dad. He looks smaller out here among the old growth trees. I imagine him hiking around out here in the dark. Alone except for Carol, flung over his shoulder like a sack of potatoes. "Not even you."

"Good Lord, son. Maybe you ought to talk to someone about that. It seems to me that if anybody would have enough pent up rage to off someone, it should be you."

I look around for the nearest officer and raise my hand. He starts the short climb up the hill toward us. The officer stops a few paces away. "You done here?"

"I sure am."

Dad's face drops. "We haven't gotten to Carol's body yet. Don't you want to know where she's at?"

"Nope." I stomp back down the hill toward the patrol car feeling a bit like a pissed off teenager who is refusing to take out the garbage.

"Well if he won't listen to me, I guess I'll just have to tell you, Officer," Dad shouts, talking to the cop but wanting me to hear.

I cover my ears and keep marching, willing myself to not look back. I won't let him use this woman's deteriorating corpse against me. Yes, I want to be the hero and recover her body. For her family. For her children. I spit on the ground beside the black and white car.

"Have a goddamned contest?" I mutter to myself. "Fuck."

I don't look back up the hill until I am in the front seat of the car with the door closed. Once I move my gaze back up, I see him watching me. He stands apart from the swarm of officers that are now digging in the ground, about ten yards from where we were just talking. Dad stares down at me a moment longer. He has a look of disappointment cemented on his face.

It shouldn't make my heart drop when he turns his back on me. But it does.

Dougy slides into the car beside me a few minutes later and straps himself in. "They found Carol. Well, her foot, anyway. I'll take you home before we start really getting into the scene. Unless you want to take a look?"

I shake my head. "Not interested, thanks. But could you drop me off somewhere else?"

"Sure." He turns the key and the engine roars to life. "Where to?"

"14th and Burnside." I pull my buckle into place just as Dougy drives over the root from a nearby tree, rocking the car hard.

Dougy looks at me sideways as the car bottoms out in a dip in the dirt road. "What do you guys talk about when you are out there, anyway?"

"Murder, mostly."

The Inspector breaks out in laughter as if I have just told the world's funniest joke. I lay my head against the cool glass of the window and close my eyes. Jeanne will help. She always does.

# Break

"I talked to my dad." Jeanne seemed distracted when I first came in, but this snaps her attention toward me.

"How is that going?"

"OK, I guess. He's asked me to work on a job with him and I sort of volunteered." Jeanne looks at me, confused. "It's similar to work release."

"Isn't that interesting?" Jeanne taps her pen against her chin. "What kind of job is your dad doing for his work release?"

I think about the last two weeks in the woods looking for Carol and my dad's offer to give up another body along I-5 in Southwest Washington.

"You know those crews that work on the side of the highway, picking up trash and cutting back weeds?" Jeanne nods at me. "Well, that's sort of what it is. Except it's not just inmates, but also volunteers."

Jeanne smiles as she makes a note on her pad of paper. "That is a step forward, isn't it?"

I nod happily at her. She shifts in her seat as she looks back over her notes. "What about work? How are you fitting this new volunteer position in with your day job?"

"I took a leave of absence."

"You must be really dedicated to getting those highways cleaned up to take a break from work."

"It seemed like to make this thing with my dad work, I should probably give it my full attention."

Jeanne beams at me and I can feel her pride at my ability to come to these conclusions on my own. She mumbles softly as she writes, "Progress, indeed." There is a momentary pause as she collects her thoughts. "How is Elsie handling this transition?"

I wish that Jeanne would stop bringing Elsie up all the time. "I still haven't told her."

I watch the pride dissolve into a frown. "Peter, honesty is a vital part of a healthy relationship. I'm concerned about how many important life changes you are tackling without giving her the chance to offer her support."

"It would be too much for her." I stammer, "With a full course load and the holidays coming up. I can't burden her with this stuff."

"It is very sweet of you to try to protect her from this tumultuous situation, but eventually she will find out that you aren't working. Wouldn't you rather that she find out from you than from someone else?"

"She doesn't have to find out, Jeanne."

"But don't you think that once you've reconnected with your father that you'll want the two of them to meet?" Jeanne dangles the possibility of a normal family in front of me. A carrot suspended in front of a lonely mule.

I look deep into her dark green eyes. "Absolutely not."

# Discovery

We've walked through the miniature forest on the median of I-5 just outside of Kalama, Washington for three days. Dad insists that he left David here. Either his memory is faulty this time, or the body has been moved. The thick trees that fill the space between the north and southbound lanes of the Washington Interstate make it look as if there hasn't been any construction since his last visit but it's obvious that the wildlife and homeless populations use the brush cover frequently.

Dad is locked up in the back of a Search and Rescue car in Dougy's futile attempt to force more memory out of him. I stand on the hill watching as officers with scent dogs pass over the quarter mile stretch. The way the dogs work is fascinating. I hope that one of them picks up the scent of a cadaver soon so that I can witness the end of their hunt.

The traffic has been awful today, probably owing to the flashing police lights and dogs alongside the interstate. It's been mostly stop and go, so by the time I notice the silver car pulled off to the far shoulder on the northbound lane I have no idea how long it has been sitting there. I stare in disbelief at the tiny blonde woman perched on the hood with a laptop balanced on her knees.

"Is everything OK?" Dougy pops into my peripheral.

"Yeah. I think that might be my girlfriend." I point at her and her face shies away from me.

"I thought we agreed that you wouldn't tell anyone about this? These searches have to be kept confidential, Pete. For the families."

"I didn't tell her anything." I glare at him. "Fuck, Dougy. After all these years, the least you could do is give me a little credit."

"Well then what is she doing here?"

"I don't know." Despite the mist that clings to my face, I'm starting to get warm.

"Let's go find out."

We start across the median and Elsie scrambles off her hood. She fumbles when she tries to slide her laptop into its carrying case, which buys us enough time to reach the edge of the highway. In a rare moment of usefulness Dougy holds out his badge and the cars that creep along the lanes in front of us come to a stop. We cross the freeway and are standing beside her car before she can get the door shut.

"Ma'am, I am Senior Inspector Douglas." He

78

pushes his badge at her.

"Shut up, Dougy." I look down at Elsie's startled face. "What. The. Fuck."

"Oh, hi." Elsie pushes her hair behind her ears and the sound of air sucking past her teeth amplifies her nervous vibe.

"What the hell are you doing out here?"

Elsie looks across the interstate at the median. "You didn't show up at work this morning, so I went to your apartment. I saw you leave in a cop car and I just -"

"*Dispatch to Charlie 37. We have a possible break-in at 7723 West 25th. Please respond.*"

I yank Elsie's door open and lean over her. "Is that a fucking police scanner?"

Elsie smiles at me and shrinks back in her seat. "I just wanted to make sure you were OK. The scanner said something about cadaver dogs and I -"

"You have got to be shitting me." I punch the radio perched on her dashboard until it turns off. I feel Dougy's hand on me, and I back out of the car. I pace back and forth a few times before I look at her again. "Are you following me?"

Her eyes narrow and she spits, "Yeah. I am. Somebody has to. You're out here digging up bodies

79

and nobody knows where the hell you are, or what you're doing. And when it comes out that you've got that asshole father of yours traipsing around the freeway you're going to need somebody on your side to tell your story."

Dougy's eyes go wide. "Wait. You're that KRTF fact-checker that stopped by my office a few months ago, aren't you?"

I look at him and back at Elsie. "Fact checker?"

Dougy points at Elsie, "She came into my office with a news badge and a long list of questions about your dad. Wanted to know how many more bodies we had to recover and whether or not you had agreed to help us out."

I feel like I've just been punched in the stomach and all the air whooshes out of me at once. I lean over, hands on my knees, trying to get the world to stop spinning. Finally I squawk, "We've been dating a year."

Now it's Dougy's turn to be thrown back in shock. "You what? You're dating someone from the media? What the literal fuck is this, Henry? If I would have known, none of this would have ever happened. Holy shit. You've got the goddamned evening news sleeping in your bed, and you're pissed at me for coming to your apartment in case someone figures out who you are?"

"We never slept together." Elsie bursts out of her car and looks ready for a fight. "Our relationship was purely professional. We were only together so that I could break the story. Nothing unsavory ever happened between us."

"Unsavory?" I stand, look up at the dark Washington sky and laugh. "I'm so glad that your decorum has been upheld to such a professional standard."

"Look, Petey, I just wanted to get your side of the story." Elsie moves toward me with the soft face she uses whenever she wants me to cave in. "They told me that if I brought an earth shattering story in that I could get off of my desk. I could be on camera for the first time. What story could be bigger than a son trying to right his father's wrongs?"

"Maybe you could have asked me for the story instead of pretending to be my goddamn girlfriend." I look at Dougy and yell, "I didn't know she was a reporter. I thought she was a student at PSU. Apparently, I don't know a damn thing about this crossed legged prude of a bitch."

Dougy nods at me and grabs Elsie by the arm. "Miss, you're going to have to come with me."

Elsie screeches like a madwoman. I don't know how he does it, but Dougy manages to hold on to her writhing body. Without losing his grip, he gets the cuffs out of his belt-pouch and onto her wrists as they fly through the air at him.

"My editor is expecting to hear from me in twenty minutes. If he doesn't hear from me, he'll call the authorities."

I've never seen Dougy look so much like an actual cop. "Miss, I am the authorities."

Dougy pawns Elsie, or whatever her name is, off on another officer. He starts searching her car, pulling out stacks of papers and recording devices. He's got an evidence box half-filled when he realizes I'm still standing there, watching. "Henry, you'd better get back across the road to the median. Maybe your dad is ready to talk. That is, if you're up to it."

I look at the world around me. Dozens of cars are stopped, filled with regular people who sit in shock and wait to see what will happen next. My dad still sits in the back of the patrol car across the freeway, but now the door is open and he puffs on a cigarette. He looks as if he's watching a rerun of his favorite soap opera. Cops shout at each other while dogs bark just inside the tree line of the median. *"We've got a torso,"* crackles out of the earbud that hangs loosely along Dougy's sweaty face.

I'm in the middle of the most fucked up three-ring circus there ever was. "Sure Dougy, I'll talk to him. At least I know who the hell he is."

I stomp back toward my dad without looking at the cars that start to inch forward again as I pass. When I get to him, I spin around and lean against the rear quarter panel. I cross my arms against my chest with a huff.

"That your girlfriend?" Dad points with the cigarette at the patrol car across the freeway where Elsie is bouncing around in the back seat like a cracked out Chihuahua.

"She was."

"It doesn't appear things are going too well."

"Certainly doesn't."

Dad looks up at me with a half amused smile. "It's almost enough to make a man go mad and kill someone. Don't you think?"

"Shut up, Dad."

# Contest

I walk out to a spot near where we found Carol's body. I have no idea what I'm looking for, but somehow being out here makes me feel closer to my dad. I Look over the woods where we spent so many summers exploring, and where he spent decades hiding his secrets, I realize that he is right. He wasn't just a crazy homicidal maniac. He was someone who always knew just what to do. He was a guy who no one pushed around. He was someone who would be remembered.

Maybe it wouldn't be terrible to be more like him.

My sigh is absorbed by the wind as it blows through the trees. I have to figure out what to do. I think for half a second about going after Elsie and reenacting my mother's murder with her. After all she's done to me I don't think anyone would be surprised if I showed up at the news station and went on a rampage. I try to picture Elsie sprawled out on the forest floor, but I can't decide if she'd look better with a knife sticking out of her chest or a noose slung around her neck. I shrug the image off. I don't think I could ever kill someone so violently. Not even Elsie.

I try to think of some way that I can experience

whatever warped sense of accomplishment that Dad keeps talking about without being forced to watch someone die. I'd rather be responsible for someone's death through inaction than by pushing their last breath out of them. I've already done that countless times. After all, isn't that what I did every time Dad invited one of those people over for dinner? Deep down I knew when I looked across the table at those people spooning heaps of Mom's mashed potatoes into their hungry mouths that we'd never see them again. But I never whispered any warnings or showed them out the back door when Dad wasn't in the room.

I look down at my hands and it suddenly occurs to me that I'm already a killer. I've been one for as long as I've been old enough to set the table.

I think back on Dad's suggestion to make a cracker-jack contest. At the time, the thought of setting some kid up to open up a box and die seemed unfathomable. But I wouldn't have to kill a kid. Maybe I could have some genuinely awesome prizes for the kids and save death for the weird cat ladies and basement dwelling bachelors. Sure. I could just wait for someone who would try to game the system to add toys to their porno-funding eBay page.

I mull this over for a minute. The simplicity of

the idea evaporates. Do they even make Cracker Jacks any more? And even if they do, don't the prizes always come inside the box? I don't know how to selectively place some nefarious prize inside a box of treats and then make sure that the right person gets it.

Exhausted, I slump down against a tree. The dampness on the ground sucks into my jeans. Soon, I'm wet and shivering. I think about how Carol died. Dad met her somewhere in town and they had gotten into a debate about religion. He invited her over for dinner so that she could see with her own eyes the peace and love that comes from a faith-based family. How anyone so preachy could convince perfect strangers to come to a family dinner was still beyond me. But she had come to enjoy some of Mom's great food and had smiled when I talked about school. After dinner she remained seated at the table to discuss theology with Dad over coffee. I'd told her it was nice to meet her before going up to bed. The next time I'd seen Carol's face was on a missing persons flier at the grocery store.

Tears fill my eyes and I let them fall freely since no one is around to watch. I cry for all the people who still lay out in the woods waiting to be discovered. I cry for my mother, who died because she loved me so much that she wanted to make Dad stop so that I could have the life of a normal kid. I cry for my dad who was so invested in saving the lost souls of the world that he couldn't stop.

The only person I don't cry for is me. I won't feel sorry for myself today. For once, I will stop blaming everyone around me for my misery. After all of these years of trying to be normal, I'm going to give in and embrace who I really am.

I just need to find the right way.

## Bad Advice

"So, how are things?" Jeanne beams up at me as I shuffle into the room. I slump down in the chair across from her. I wish I had the energy to reflect the happiness in her eyes.

"Everything's fucked up."

Jeanne looks at me with soft round eyes. My bad mood is going to run over her like a semi-truck. "I'm sorry to hear that. Care to embellish a bit?"

"Elsie and I broke up." I pull at the collar of my shirt. The soft cotton is suffocating me.

"From some of the things you've told me about your relationship with her the last few weeks, I can't say that I'm really surprised. What was it that finally clinched it?"

I look up at the ceiling. I can't look Jeanne in the eye. "Ugh. Who knows. We were ships passing in the night. Isn't that what people say when it just doesn't work out?"

"Yes. But relationships don't usually end for no reason. There's usually a catalyst that clenches things. I'm sure you and Elsie had yours. If you don't want to talk about it, I am happy to respect that."

The formal tone that Jeanne uses makes me

feel she'll be upset with me if I don't tell her something. I want her to be happy again. "Elsie wasn't who I thought she was."

"Figuratively, or literally?"

"Literally." I snap my gaze down from the ceiling and look Jeanne in the eye. "She was a damn prostitute. I never had a clue."

"Well," Jeanne sighs. "That certainly explains her distance with you, doesn't it?"

I love that no matter what I tell her, Jeanne doesn't challenge me. She just takes my word as it is. Sure, she asks clarifying questions. She couldn't call herself a therapist if she didn't. But her questions always make me want to give her more. They don't put me on the defensive. Finally, I smile at Jeanne.

"So, have you had yourself checked out?" The arch in her right eyebrow lifts a centimeter. I long to run my finger along the short hairs and kiss her brow.

"Checked out for what?"

"You know, for STD's. If you've been with a woman for a year who has been selling her body to other men, you probably should talk to your physician if you haven't already."

"Oh, right. Yeah, I went to the doctor right away. I'm just waiting for the results to come back."

89

My fingers twitch so I fold my hands together in my lap. "I'm sure it will all be fine. We weren't really very..."

"Intimate?" Jeanne offers. Her eyelashes wave at me and I can make out a slight blush on her cheeks when she says the word. I imagine she's thinking of me being intimate with Elsie, and that makes me blush, too.

"Yeah, intimate. Elsie didn't do anything with me like that. I guess she didn't think I was that attractive."

"It sounds to me as if she may have been using you." Jeanne jots a quick note.

"I think that's safe to assume." I grunt.

"Did you spend a lot of money on her?"

I think back on the few outings that Elsie and I made together. "I bought a lot of dinner, mostly. A person has to eat."

"What do you think she wanted from you?" Jeanne looks puzzled. I can tell that she had expected me to say I'd done a lot more for Elsie than buy her food.

"My identity." I make it a point to rub the wallet in my front pocket.

"Did she steal your credit cards?"

I lift my chin up in agreement. "Ran them up

90

good. She bought all kinds of kinky shit for her clients, I guess. Whatever she bought, it didn't do me any good, anyway."

Jeanne frowns. "I'm really sorry to hear that Elsie and you didn't work out. What is your plan now?"

"I still have this volunteer stuff going with my dad."

"Oh, yes. How are things going with him?"

I glance up at the clock. "He wants me to work on a project with him. I've never done it before, and I don't know if I want to."

"What kind of project is it?"

I look around the room nervously. I can't bring myself to say it, so I blurt out the next best thing. "Taxidermy."

"Taxidermy?" Jeanne seems genuinely surprised, and I give her a nervous smile.

"I mentioned before that it was kind of my dad's hobby before he got arrested. He was really good at it, and he wants me to be good at it, too."

Jeanne nods. "It's an art form, from what little I understand. But it doesn't seem to be something that would be easy to take on."

I shake my head. "No, it sure isn't. All the preparation is really what gets to me. I mean, maybe if

91

I was in the middle of it, I would be able to figure it out. But getting started. It's just so..."

"Gory?"

"Yeah. Gory. I don't know if I can stomach it."

"Well, Peter. I guess there's only one question to ask yourself. Do you really want to reconnect with your father?"

I nod.

"Then, do you think you can manage to give taxidermy a try?"

I look down at the floor and nod again.

## Sasha

Dad and I walk around the parking lot of the Oregon Trail Interpretive Center outside of Baker City. The early November air bites at my neck and I pull the collar of my coat up to keep the wind off. Dad walks around in his jumpsuit and a light jacket, oblivious to the fact that the thermometer reads two degrees above freezing.

He hasn't said what kind of marker we're supposed to look for. He did promise the group of U.S. Marshals scattered around the property that we'll find Sasha here. She was a twenty-something office assistant when she was last seen. That was almost thirty years ago.

"I'm going to try things your way." I speak low, but with the way the wind howls around us I doubt anyone outside of arm's reach would be able to hear me even if I were shouting.

"Oh?" Dad stops walking and looks at me with surprise. "Do you mean..."

I nod once and know that he understands. He smiles and I duck a little further into my jacket. Just because I've decided to do this for him doesn't mean that I have to feel good about it.

"Do you know how you'll do it?" He moves a little closer and suddenly acts chilled. I put my arm around him.

"No. Well, maybe. I don't know." I shake a little, as we talk about it. Dad pushes up closer against me and gives me a nudge of understanding.

"The planning and anticipation are the worst part," he offers. "Once you've done it a few times – get a system down – then it gets a lot easier."

I back off from him abruptly. "Shit, Dad. Calm down. I said I'd try it out, not blaze the trail for a whole new generation of career killers."

"Sorry." He shrugs. "Was just trying to let you know that I understand how hard it is to get started."

I get close to him again. "How did you do it the first time?"

Dad laughs. "She just fell into my lap. I never did learn her name. I was running away from home for the millionth time. She got onto the bus, drunk and mean. An old lady was sitting across the aisle from me and the drunk woman wanted her to give the seat up because she was having trouble standing. The old lady got pissed and whacked her in the head with her purse. Knocked her clean out. She fell on me. She smelled like turpentine and she had a swastika tattooed on her

94

neck. I could tell she was a bad person."

The wind gusts, pushing us a little further toward the edge of the top tier of the parking lot. We let it carry us a few feet and then resume our slow, circular walk around the perimeter. I glance over the collar of my jacket to make sure no one has noticed the added distance between us and the group. "Then what?"

"She was out cold. When no one was looking, I shoved her tongue down her throat."

"Holy fuck, Dad. How did you know to do that?"

Dad shrugged. "When your granddaddy used to get stumbling down drunk, Mammy used to make us roll him on his side and check his tongue when he passed out.

"So you didn't plan out your first one?"

"Nope. It just happened. But that's when I knew what God put me on this earth to do. Watching her laying on her back, dying alone, it was the most peace I'd ever felt."

"And you didn't get caught?"

He shakes his head and grins. "They all just blamed it on her being drunk. Nobody figured out what was happening until it was too late. Besides, who's going to blame a ten year old for killing some lady on

95

the bus?"

"You were ten? Jesus Christ."

Dad looks at me with a glimmer in his eye. "Don't use the Lord's name in vain, son. He doesn't like it."

I look up into the gray sky above us. "Sorry, Jesus."

"Don't be patronizing."

"So, do you think it will be that easy for me?" I probably look more hopeful than I should.

"Not everyone is that lucky, son." Dad gives me a quick hug under my jacket. "Besides, as an adult there's a lot more to think about. You've got to make sure that you arrange events in such a way that it doesn't come back on you."

Dougy suddenly appears from behind us. I pop my head up and look around. We've drifted past the wagons circled on the edge of the hill, almost out of eyesight of the parking lot. "Oh, sorry. I didn't realize how far we'd gotten from the group. That wind."

Dougy looks at me suspiciously, but then nods when a gust blows him back a foot. He comes closer and talks to Dad. "Ollie, you've got to let us know what we're looking for. It's freezing out here and we're just walking around in circles looking at scrub brush."

Dad nods. "You know what? I just remembered. They probably don't keep her out here."

Dougy and I look at each other, confused.

"The elements," Dad gestures to the world around us, "would probably deteriorate it too quickly. I guess with how much they paid for it, they probably would want to take better care of it than that."

"What in the hell are you talking about?" Dougy looks like he's about to lose it.

Dad gives him a calm smile. "As I think about it, I figure a museum that spent eight thousand dollars on a stuffed bear probably keeps it on display somewhere inside. Don't you think?"

"A bear?" Dougy and I ask in unison.

"I don't know how happy they'll be with you ripping it apart, it having been so expensive and all. But if you put the Grizzly through an x-ray machine, you might find what you're looking for."

Dougy slaps his forehead with the palm of his hand. He calls another marshal over and instructs him to take Dad back to the room they rented in town until they verify Sasha's location. If there's a bear in the museum with a body in it, they'll send him straight back to his cell in Sheridan.

"Good luck," Dad calls over his shoulder at me

97

as they drag him away. "And don't forget to have a little fun with it!"

# Breakfast

I mindlessly stir my spoon in a bowl of Alphabet Apes. It's been a week since Baker City and I haven't been able to stop thinking about murder. The doing it, the not doing it, and all of the ramifications of either situation. Dad is right about me. I've spent my whole life trying to be a simple, normal person. But how could I ever be normal? Everything about who I am is fucked to the hilt. I decide I'll at least plan out a murder. I won't have to go all the way through it. Maybe just setting someone up will get me close enough to understand all of the things my dad tells me. Maybe it will make me see the world the way he sees it.

The idea shoots through me in a flash. I push myself away from the table and snatch my grocery list off the side of my refrigerator and click the top of a ball point pen. I flip the list over to a blank page and start to write. I don't stop until the cereal is so soggy that it's started to glob together and I've got four pages of notes.

I'll do a cereal prize giveaway. I can print up some fake prize codes and wait for someone to call. I'll come up with some legitimate prizes and if anyone I don't like turns up to collect their winnings, I'll award them with an axe to the face. I wince a little at the image painted in my head. Maybe not an axe.

I take the sheets of rambling thoughts and look for a safe place to keep them. I settle on putting them under my socks in the dresser. When I close the drawer I keep my hands on the handles. Relief pours out of me and I close my eyes as every tense muscle relaxes. Now that I know what I'm going to do, it's just as Dad described. I feel a kind of peace I haven't ever felt before.

I collapse on the bed, a smile on my face. My cheeks ache from the effort, but the fact that I'm able to smile just makes the expression expand. I close my eyes and let the peace wash over me. I melt into the mattress and I feel myself falling into sleep.

It's almost dark by the time I wake up again. A storm howls outside and it looks like midnight even though it's hardly a quarter to five. I rub the sleep out of my eyes and turn my head to glance at the dresser. I feel a connection to it that is different from anything I've ever had for another person. I get up and caress the top of the drawer that holds my secret. It's odd the way the wood grain seems to lean up against my palm like a cat stretching into its owner's hand.

I open the closet and pull out a dark hooded sweatshirt. I tug it on over my head and march out of the room, grabbing my keys off the coffee table as I make my way to the front door. I turn the knob to lock it and for the first time since I've lived here don't have the urge to double check it when the door slams closed behind me.

My windshield wipers have a hard time keeping up with the rain. As much as I am ready to barrel down the road to the bank, I know if I get into an accident now it will delay the entire project. Even with the downpour it's only a fifteen minute drive. I walk into the sparsely populated lobby, glad I made it in before closing. The teller nods at me and I have to hold myself back from skipping to his counter.

"Good evening. Can I help you?"

I try to return his professional smile but judging from the startled look on the teller's face I realize I must look like a crazy person. Lord knows I feel like one.

I pass him my bank card and drivers license. "I want to withdraw the balance of my savings."

"I'd be happy to help you with that, Mr. Wilson. Let me just pull up your account."

I glance down at the man's nametag. "Thank you, Sam."

There is a flourish of fingers on the keyboard,

and Sam's face screws to the left. He bites the inside of his cheek and his eyes flit back over to me. "Mr. Wilson, you've done a great job building up this savings account. Unfortunately, I don't think we have the balance available in cash just now. Can you wait a minute while I get my manager?"

I nod. I hadn't considered that the bank wouldn't have twenty thousand dollars stashed in the vault. I stomp my foot, impatient with my inability to think ahead to something as important as this. I see Sam whisper to a woman near the back of the bank. She nods at him and approaches me with a wide smile. Even from across the lobby I can tell that she pays way too much attention to her dental hygiene. Her teeth glow from behind her muted red lips and I feel compelled to force a carafe of coffee past them to make them less perfect.

"Mr. Wilson. Such a pleasure to see you this evening. Do you mind if we discuss your withdrawal in my office?"

I follow her into a small windowless room and she clicks the door closed behind me. I sit in one of two cheaply upholstered chairs while she wiggles her plump body past the narrow opening alongside her desk. She makes it to her chair without knocking anything over and then settles into the leather. She leans forward and folds her hands on the desk top.

"Sam tells me that you want to withdraw the balance of your savings this evening. Is there anything that we can do to keep your funds here at the bank?"

I look around the office for a plaque or sign with the woman's name. This must be a generic office that the entire staff uses though. There isn't a single personalized trinket anywhere. "If you don't mind my asking, who are you?"

She laughs a too-loud laugh. "Forgive me. I'm Valorie Scruggins. Manager of this branch. Now, about that withdrawal..."

"I'm not switching to another bank," I announce.

Valorie's voice lilts nervously. "Well that is certainly good to hear. With the quantity of your request, I had worried that we've done something to offend you."

"This has been a great bank." I lean forward. "But I still need to get my savings."

"You must be making quite the purchase. Has anyone talked to you about our competitive auto loans and mortgage rates?"

I start to get agitated. "It's more of an

103

investment thing, Valorie. Not something I need a loan for since I have cash on hand. I'm sure you understand."

"Oh, I certainly do!" Valorie pulls a piece of paper out of a stack of office supplies on the edge of the desk. A pen appears from the inside pocket of her blazer and she makes a note. Valorie is not as graceful a note taker as Jeanne. "Unfortunately, in this day of electronic transactions we just don't keep that much money on hand any more. The best I can do is a five thousand dollar withdrawal. Then I can send a request to our main branch to send the rest of the funds by the end of the week. Is that acceptable?"

I nod. Although I'd feel better with my money in hand now, it's not as if there isn't plenty I can get done with five thousand dollars. "How will I know when the rest of the money is ready?"

Valorie hands me a business card with one of six phone numbers circled. "It will be here by Friday afternoon. Just give me a call before you head down and I'll make sure that it is stacked and counted for you by the time you get here."

I take the card from her and she picks up the phone to relay instructions to the teller out front to bring me the five thousand. "In twenties," I ask. She

104

repeats my request into the phone.

"It will be just a few minutes." Valorie makes herself busy sorting the post-its so they'll be ready for the next person who drags a customer in here. Her eyebrow raises and she steals a glance at me.

"You look like you want to ask me a question." I can feel the corner of my mouth rise a bit in a smile. The sensation catches me off guard.

Valorie's giggle reminds me of the cheerleaders I never got the chance to date in high school. "It's just that we don't usually handle cash transactions this big. Sure we do a lot of certified checks and wires, just not cash. It feels a bit like a bank robbery, doesn't it?"

"I don't know. I've never been in a bank robbery."

Valorie erupts in girlish laughter and her cheeks flush. "Oh, wow. You are funny, Mr. Wilson."

"Please, call me Peter." I try to look cool because I think Valorie is flirting with me. "Hey, will you be working on Friday?"

She blushes deeper. "Of course. What kind of manager would I be if I took Friday off to have fun while everyone else has to work?"

"Are you a coffee drinker?"

"Well, sure." She stutters a little when she

105

answers.

"When I call you to arrange picking up the rest of the money, why don't you bring it to me at the coffee shop at the corner?"

Her eyelashes dance when she bats her eyes at me. "Bring it to you?"

"Sure. You can bring a briefcase full of money to me for the hand-off. It'll be just like a high-roller deal in the movies."

Valorie's blush starts to extend down her neck and into her ample cleavage. I can see her breath quicken. She considers it for a minute and then gushes, "Well, in the movies the person dropping off the cash gets payment in return."

"True."

"So what are you going to get me?" Valorie leans against the desk seductively.

"Whatever you want." I give her my best secret-agent wink and then add, "As long as it's on the coffee shop menu and the total is less than fifteen bucks. I'm not made of money, you know."

Valorie and I laugh together. She jumps when the office door swings open and Sam comes in with an envelope that looks ready to burst. It takes him a second to pick up the flirtatious vibe in the room, then

106

he shoots me a look that says he's been trying to get Valorie to giggle like that since his first interview.

Valorie stands, smoothes her jacket and straightens her collar. She snatches the envelope from Sam and hands it to me as if she's a maiden handing me a sacrificial offering. I take it in both hands to feel the weight of it, then stick it into the front pocket of my sweatshirt without counting it.

"Until we meet again." I bow to Valorie. Then I wink at Sam, who is easily as flushed red as she is, but not because he feels flirtatious.

"I look forward to our meeting on Friday, Peter." She does her best to sound professional but she twirls her hair in her fingers and her smile this time is as genuine as it is broad.

# The Gift of Giving

I take advantage of the constant rain. I pull a baseball cap down low on my head and walk into the grocery store. I search the aisles briefly until I find the tall kiosk full of preloaded gift cards. I don't want to seem overly suspicious and with the holidays coming I know I can buy at least a handful of the Visa gift cards without anyone noticing. I select a stack of fifty and hundred dollar cards and head back to the register.

I fidget as I wait my turn. Even though I know that it's crazy, I feel the check out girl watching me. I almost bolt out of line to put the cards back on the rack but another woman touches my arm.

"I'm open on lane two. You can come with me if you don't want to wait."

I follow the woman in silence until she stands behind the register and I hand her my stack of cards. I count them all up – the total will be nine hundred and fifty dollars. Maybe I'm doing too much all at once. I should put some of them back.

"Looks like somebody's going to have a nice Christmas."

I give a blank stare while her words sink in. Finally it all clicks. I hand her my stack of hundred dollar bills. "Kids, you know."

She looks up from activating the cards and smiles. "You must have a lot of kids."

"Oh, they aren't mine." A nervous laugh pushes out of my chest. I think quickly. "Nieces and Nephews. I would just send them the cash, but nobody wants to go pick out a toy at the store any more."

The clerk chuckles. Her black hair bounces off of her shoulders and her cheeks lift so high on her face that her eyes squint when she smiles.

"Besides, you can't download iTunes with a twenty dollar bill." I rock back on my feet and give an animated shrug. The check-out girl hands me the cards and our hands touch. We smile at one another for a second too long.

She snaps back to the moment with a jump. "Oh! I almost forgot to give you all of these receipts. Each of these lines shows your activation information. Hold onto them and come back to see me if for some reason one of the cards doesn't work."

"Can I come back even if they all do?"

Customers from the lane beside us peek over the partition when she laughs again. She notices the extra attention and ducks down behind the register a little to escape the embarrassment. "You are welcome

109

back any time, Mister..."

"Ryan." I smile. She repeats the name and we bid one another farewell. I fight the urge to ask for her number. She's cute, but I've got work to do.

As I drive back across town I pass by a giant office supply store. The bad weather has shorted out part of the sign and now it blinks into the darkness the words "Off ax". I start to pull into the strip mall but then realize that I've got to do a good job of spacing my purchases out. If anyone gets suspicious, I don't want them to be able to pull security tape from all around town on the same day. It would make it too easy for them to build a case against me.

Instead, I roll down the window at a stop light. The rain spits at me, hitting me in the side of the face with cold fingers. I reach into the shopping bag and retrieve all of the receipts from the prepaid Visas. I take a quick glimpse around to make sure no one has pulled up to the intersection and then dump the slips of paper out the window. The rain saturates the paper instantly and it falls to the pavement in a heap of wet pulp.

When I get home, I pull the couch out into a bed and deposit the cards on the mattress. I pull the sheets down tight around them so that they won't slip around too much and then push the mattress back into

110

the sofa and re-arrange the cushions. My task complete, I head back to the bedroom where I know my list is waiting for me.

Warmth seems to drip from the dresser handles. I realize that the moist heat is from me, dripping wet from being out in the weather. I decide I don't want to get the list wet, so I back away for a minute and strip off all the soggy clothing and dry my hands on a shirt peeking out of the hamper. Standing in my t-shirt and boxers, I suddenly feel like I'm standing in front of a woman I'm about to make love to for the first time.

I adjust myself and take a deep breath. When I open it, the list looks up at me from the bottom of the dresser drawer. I draw it out gently, careful not to bend the pages. I take a black marker from my desktop and cross out the first line.

Crossing *Buy Prepaid Cards With Cash* off the list should just be another boring act. But it isn't. I am filled with such excitement that my hand shakes. I feel my boxers grow a little tighter and I snap the cap back onto the marker and toss it on the desk. I place the list tenderly back into the drawer.

I think about the dark haired clerk and close my eyes. I can feel her swoon under my confident gaze. Her chest heaves as I kiss her and soon her naked ass ripples while I thrust into her. She looks over her shoulder at me and suddenly she is Valorie from the bank. Her eyes are filled with the urgency of lust and she gets down on her knees to clean the wetness of sex off of me with her tongue.

I explode onto the carpet. My orgasm brings me falling to my knees and although I'd normally be complete, my hand keeps pumping. I look back at the dresser and think about the list. A second pulse stings through my groin and I lose myself again.

When I come back to my senses, I lie on the floor in the middle of my bedroom. Rain soaked clothes are strewn all around me. I pick up my damp pants from the pile and use them to mop up the sticky mess I've left in the carpet.

I curse at myself as I clean up. I don't understand how I've become such a freak. I turn off the light and try to close the door on my own shame. I decide that tonight, I'll sleep on the couch.

# Encouragement

Jeanne's leg, the one that is crossed atop the other, bobs up and down. Her flat heeled shoe dangles off of her toes as if it's holding on for dear life. She's wearing brown stockings so thin that I can see the tiny imperfections in the skin around her ankle. I wish I could reach out, draw her delicate feet into my lap, and massage them until she melts.

"So, you mentioned that you've been learning a bit about taxidermy?"

I wish she wasn't always in such a rush to pull me from my thoughts. "Yes. I've done some research. It turns out it's one of those things you can just learn at home at your own pace."

"Oh, I am so glad to hear that. So many of the people I talk to say that they want to do something but then don't follow through. I actually pulled some information on free online classes for you so I could try to encourage you to look into it further." Jeanne pulls out a manila folder that holds a thick sheaf of papers. She starts to toss it into the recycle bin beside her.

"Even though I've already got some stuff down, I'm happy to take a look at that, Jeanne." The folder is diverted and soon I hold her token of affection. She

113

must have spent time on all of this research because she cares about me. She wants me to succeed and my heart thumps in my chest as I silently promise her that I will.

"So tell me about how you are doing. Have you talked to your father?"

"We got together a couple of times for that work party, but I haven't seen him this week."

"How long until he will be fully released?" Jeanne writes a note. I wonder if she expects me to introduce her to him. He isn't exactly the kind of parent most girls would want their boyfriends to introduce them to, but Jeanne has such an interest in people and family drama that I bet she would enjoy it.

"I'm not sure. They pulled him off of work crew because-" I have to stop and think of a reason aside from *they found the body and he hasn't offered another one*. "Budget cuts."

"Oh, my. And here you have taken all this time away from work just so that you could volunteer with him. That probably doesn't seem very fair."

Jeanne really thinks things through. That's one of the things that I appreciate most about her. She has a way of putting herself in someone else's shoes and deducing how they might feel in a situation. If volunteering to see my dad had been the only reason I

114

had taken time off work, I'm sure I really would be disappointed. "No, Jeanne. It doesn't seem fair at all."

"So what will you do? Go back to work?"

"No. I think I'll focus on this taxidermy stuff for a while. Maybe if I really put my time into it, I'll be able to have the basics down before I have to go back to my cubicle."

Jeanne makes another note, and then looks me in the eye. She looks so deep that I can feel her search my soul. "You know, when people with a criminal past are released with a plan and support network, they can go on to be very productive members of society. I commend you for taking an interest in your father's talents. I think it will serve him well when he is trying to re-integrate into normal life."

I laugh a little. "I don't know that my dad will ever be normal. He's a little weird."

Jeanne smiles. "Everybody's a little weird, Peter."

"Not everyone." I feel my skin flush. "You aren't weird."

She laughs with such fervor that she throws her head back. Her hair cascades behind her, stroking the back of her chair. Her whole body goes through waves of tenseness and relaxation, writhing in the ecstasy of

115

her humor. "Peter, it takes a *really* weird person to want to sit around all day listening to other people's problems."

"No," I correct her. "Just a very special one."

# Winter

I awaken to find Portland covered in a blanket of snow. It isn't even Thanksgiving yet so the serenity of the white morning is a surprise. I decide to take advantage of the cold and vacant city. As I dress, I put on a hoodie and a thick jacket. The combination is baggy and disfiguring but in the snow the attire is fitting. I pull the hood up as I head out of my apartment.

When I get to the office supply store I knock the snow off my boots at the door but keep my hood up. I hunch down a little into the sweatshirt. The generic holiday music that plays overhead is the only evidence of people – everywhere I look the store appears empty. I stroll the aisles until I find the glossy stickers and pull two packages of a hundred off the rack. I have no idea how many I will need but two hundred should be enough to get me started.

I try to think if there is anything else I'll need and decide on some double-sided sticky tape, a couple of cheap easels and large pieces of foam-backed poster board. I haul the lot up to the front registers and find them empty. I think for a minute about just walking out with the stuff. A glance at the behind the counter reveals an image of me as I stand by the counter on their closed-circuit TV.

I leave my pile of goods at the register and walk around the perimeter of the store. Finally I find a scrawny kid stocking a shelf of toilet paper in the back corner. He's all alone and although he is busy at work, it is clear that he's hiding from anyone who might come into the store. He looks barely old enough to have a job, let alone to be working all by himself at eight in the morning.

"Hey, do you think you could come ring me up?"

The kid looks at me nervously. He stammers some incoherent garbage and eventually speaks loud enough that I understand him. "... I mean, I was trained on the registers I just don't normally work up there."

"Is anyone else here?" I look back down the empty aisle behind me.

"They'll be here sometime soon." He looks up and shrugs. "The snow."

I nod. "I've really got to get going. Do you think you can give it a shot? Maybe you can get things started and when somebody else shows up they can finish."

The kid nods and gets up from his crouched

position. His nametag catches the fluorescent lights from overhead and I get a good look at it as he walks past. "Thanks, Carl."

Carl takes the longest route to the registers possible in hopes that someone will save him. I follow patiently. We round the last corner and Carl weaves from side to side as he tries to force himself behind the counter. I put my hand on his shoulder.

"It's going to be OK, Carl. I was a cashier at Mervyn's back in college. We can figure this out."

Carl raises his pimpled face to mine. "What's Mervyn's?"

I shake my head. "It doesn't matter. They had cash registers. That's what's important. Now, how do you log in?"

Carl taps the touch-screen and enters his security code. I lean over the counter and watch his fingers dance across the screen. The program is so simplistic. I have no idea why Carl stands there staring at the machine as if it might eat him.

"Maybe you could just pick up the scanner gun and point it at one of the UPC codes," I offer.

"Like when we scan stuff in for inventory?" When Carl looks at me with sad eyes I get so angry with his incompetence that I could strangle him. I shrug

119

my shoulders instead.

"I don't know, Carl. I've never done inventory."

Carl puts a shaky hand out onto the pile and pulls it away. I'm relieved that he's picked up one of the packs of labels since that's really the only thing I need. If we can just get this one package scanned and paid for, I'll feel a lot better about this whole endeavor.

After holding the package at a weird angle, Carl accidentally holds the damn barcode flat enough that the scanner sees it and the register beeps. The UPC code and description pop up on his screen followed by the item's price. "Great job, Carl. Let's see if we can get the rest of this to scan."

Carl gives me a weak shrug and glances toward the door. I've been in here nearly a half hour and nobody else has come in. It's one of the benefits of Portland. Whenever the weather shifts, everyone goes into hiding. If you're brave enough to venture outside there isn't anyone around to take notice.

I lean against the counter as casually as I can. I glance back at the security monitor and look at myself while Carl scans my purchases with painful slowness. I look easily twenty pounds heavier under the combined fluff of the sweatshirt and coat, and it's impossible to tell the color of my hair under the hood. I smile at

120

myself in the TV screen but there's something weird about the way my expression translates to film and my reflection sends back a sinister sneer.

Carl has my purchases packaged in individual plastic bags and asks if I need anything else. He shoves the poster board off the edge of the counter on accident and bends a corner when he lunges to save it. I cringe at the imperfection and then look the five nearly empty plastic bags over. Is suffocation of a sales clerk justifiable if he's useless behind a register?

"Only thing I need now is for you to take my money and run." I fish one of the hundred dollar gift cards out of my wallet and hand it over to him. He looks horrified.

"I've never run a card before."

"It's okay. We've gotten this far, right?"

I lean across the counter again and look at the screen. A giant yellow button screams "SUBTOTAL". I gesture towards it. Carl doesn't get the hint, and I'm tired of waiting. I reach over him and tap the button with the back of my knuckle. The register beeps again and my total flashes across the screen. I owe just over seventy five dollars.

Carl continues to stare ahead like a hooked carp so I carefully tap the Debit / Charge button with my knuckle and swipe the card on the reader attached to his machine. The system computes the transaction for a moment, then spits out a receipt. I sign it with the name Rayanne Higgins and hand it over to Carl. He doesn't even look at the signature and shoves the slip of paper into a slot on the side of the machine.

I walk away with my five plastic bags and two giant foam boards, glad the whole ordeal is over. Carl calls out from behind me that I've left my card. "It's just a gift card, Carl. Keep it. You earned it."

# The Hand-off

The world had frozen into a sheet of ice overnight, but by mid-morning it is thawed and soggy again. I gaze across the coffee shop, trying to keep my eye out for Valorie without making all of the people between me and the door nervous. Valorie is late. At least, I hope she is late and hasn't run off with my fifteen thousand dollars. I pound three coffees in the hour I wait for her, quickly regretting my decision. I let my gaze break from the front door in search of a bathroom. I am about to abandon my post when she sneaks in, pulling on the large glass door so gingerly that the bell above her hardly utters a tinkle. She spots me and tiptoes through the other patrons.

I get up and extend my hand to greet her. When she reaches forward she doesn't clasp my hand the way I expect, instead she twists my wrist and slaps a cold steel cuff on me.

"What the hell?" I try to back away from her but a thin chain glints at me and prevents my escape. My body tenses and I wonder if I've been figured out already.

Valorie leans in and whispers to me. "You can't just walk around with a case full of money. You've got

123

to add a little flair, don't you think?"

I look down at the end of the chain, surprised when it ends in a silver briefcase. Valorie lays it down cautiously on the small cafe table and turns it so that the combination locks face me. Her breath fills my ear as she whispers, "9-5-10".

I push my chair against the wall behind me and perch on its edge. I glance around quickly to make sure that no one watching us and then I enter the combination. Valorie drags a chair loudly to my side and we peer down at the briefcase together. The "snap-snap" of the two clasps as they spring open is one of the most electrifying sounds I've ever heard. I inch the lid up until I see the edge of five rows of five dollar bills.

My glee escapes in a quick laugh as I lift the lid further to expose another five rows of bills. The case is stacked from floor to lid with money and I have to fight the urge to pull it all out and throw it over my head like confetti. It's all my money. It came out of my bank account, after all. But just as Valorie said the last time I saw her, it does feel a little like we've pulled off a great heist.

"There's ten rows per layer, and it's three layers deep." Valorie's breath is sweet like wine and I notice her rosy cheeks for the first time. She lays her hand on my arm just above the handcuff and leans in to kiss me. The whole scene is straight out of a movie.

I lose myself in her as we kiss and am only pulled from the revelry of the moment by the sound of an impatient man clearing his throat across the table from us. I slap the lid closed and look up at him with a mixture of hope that he hasn't seen inside the case, and bashfulness at my brazen affection for this strange banker woman.

"Can I get the lady a coffee?" He puts such a grating tone on the word "lady" that his disgust at our kiss is palatable.

Valorie's once pink cheeks burn a deep crimson but she pushes past the embarrassment and commands, "I want a blueberry scone – heated. Two cake popsicles. One vanilla, one chocolate. Also, a large soy vanilla double-shot espresso latte. Add whipped cream, sprinkles and a hint of nutmeg."

The waiter rolls his eyes as he absorbs her order. "Anything else, Miss?"

"That depends. What's my total?"

The man pulls a calculator from the apron around his waist and adds the order together. "It'll be twelve dollars and thirty six cents."

"Well, I'm only allowed a fifteen dollar tab according to our deal. So..." Valorie steals a glance around the waiter at the daily special and adds, "One of those two dollar croissant rolls as well."

I hand the waiter fifteen dollars out of my wallet. He starts back across the cafe and Valorie shouts, "Thank you, Love. Keep the change!"

We snicker together over the briefcase. She strokes my arm and her intoxicated breath is once again in my ear. "I've always wanted to do that."

"Do what?" I joke. "Order half the menu, or piss off the person bringing you your food?"

"Both." Valorie presses her body against mine and kisses the nape of my neck. Her hand strokes my thigh in much the same manner that my hand caresses the briefcase of money. I suddenly realize two truths. One, that Valorie is coming back to my apartment with me. Two, that I still have to pee.

# Thanksgiving

The holidays are only enjoyed by people with family and friends, and these days I have a shortage of both commodities. Most Portlandians are traveling out to the countryside to cook organic free range turkeys in log cabins built from sustainable lumber. They'll soon stuff their faces with GMO free deviled eggs and raw sugar candied bacon. Unlike all of them, I sit in my spotless apartment snacking on a preservative-filled microwave lasagna housed in a carcinogen ridden plastic tray, watching the Macy's Day Parade on mute.

The silence of the apartment is comforting. I had a foster mother once who got me a giant boom-box and a stack of CDs for Christmas. She insisted that a life without music wasn't a life worth living. I decided that we'd have to agree to disagree and bought some sound canceling headphones so I could play the CD's with the sound turned off. It kept her off my back for about eighteen months. When she discovered that I'd spent all those hours bobbing my head to the sound of dead air, the boom box became just another bullet point on a long list of reasons she wanted me to be re-homed.

The phone rings three times before I reach it and an automated voice announces that I've received a collect call from an inmate. Would I accept the charges? I stand there with the phone pressed to my ear, trying to decide if I should hang up or not. The female voice repeats its automated message but behind it I can hear Dad shouting at me.

"You've already picked up the damn phone, Hen. If this was the answering machine it would have beeped by now. Accept the charges."

I push the star button to accept and the automated voice drops off the line. "Hey Dad. Happy Thanksgiving."

"Happy Thanksgiving, Hen." Dad sounds a little off. I can tell he's trying to sound festive, but is having a hard time getting past the steel and concrete holiday decor.

"What are you up to today?" I feel stupid as I ask the question. He's in prison and it's doubtful that the guards are itching to throw a holiday party for all of the rapists, murderers and drug traffickers housed in the Sheridan State Pen.

"Just watching the parade on TV. I am pretty sure we're having something that resembles turkey later, although it usually tastes more like sardines."

We share a silent cringe through the phone as we imagine floppy gray goop pressed into meat shapes and covered with week old gravy. I hear Dad spit on his end of the line, and I wonder how that works in prison. Wouldn't someone have to clean it up? Maybe they have prison spittoons. The Sheridan Federal Detention Center is about as far into the "Wild West" as a person can go before hitting the Pacific Ocean.

"What are you doing?" Dad asks me in return.

I look at the dim gray apartment that surrounds me. The thirty-two inch TV that I got in college is tuned to the same parade that Dad watches in his rec. room. My two dollar lasagna sits in its plastic tray, now both wilted from being overheated in the microwave and cold from sitting unattended for more than four minutes. It occurs to me that once again, Dad was right. I'm basically living the same closed-off life that he is. The only real difference is that I don't have the convenience of someone to bring me food and do my laundry.

"I was just about to step out, actually." I am pretty sure Dad knows I'm lying. He always knows. I think about being six and seeing Ted in the bottom of Dad's semi. I wonder what happened to Ted after Dad got arrested. Has someone claimed and buried him, or is he collecting dust in some macabre evidence locker? "Some friends and I are about to drive up to Mount

129

Hood for a long weekend."

"I don't blame you for wanting to take advantage of the early snow." Dad sounds dry and sarcastic. Then he clears his throat and adds, "Hey, I was wondering if you'd want to ditch out on your friends and come see your ol' Dad? There's nothing more cheerful than a prison-themed Thanksgiving."

The TV catches my eye when lights flash across the screen. A bunch of paramedics race around an ambulance parked in the middle of the parade route. The camera zooms in on a skinny hipster dangling from one of the cables attached to a giant floating Power Ranger. His arm is caught in the line. Tears stream down his face and get caught in the fluff of his meticulously groomed beard. One of the paramedics tries to help the kid down by pulling on his legs, but only succeeds in dropping his super trendy skinny jeans down around his ankles. Dad and I let out a quiet snort at the same time.

"What a jackass." I nod toward the TV as if we're sit in the room together.

"This is exactly what I was talking about a couple of weeks ago. That guy is worthless."

I roll my eyes. "Stupid yes. But worthless?"

"What kind of idiot doesn't wear a belt when

he's walking through the biggest city in the nation, on the one day that every household is watching TV?"

"I hardly think that a fashion faux pas makes a person worthless, Dad."

"Let me re-frame my statement." The kid flails wildly. People grab at the lines as they try to lower his corner of the balloon enough for him to drop down, but all he manages to do is get tangled up in the slack. The cable winds around him with the grip of a pissed off anaconda and now his face takes on a blue tinge. "What kind of jackass doesn't think to simply let go of the thing that is going to kill him?"

"Hey, from four feet off the ground, he might sprain an ankle."

Dad breaks into a full on laugh. He lets out a snort, and that gets me going, too. We laugh far beyond Skinny Jean's rescue. Through my watering eyes I watch a toned and determined EMT wave at the crowd as it goes wild around him. People pat his back and pinch his cheeks tenderly while he gives some kind of speech to the reporter who has a microphone placed conveniently under his chin. The kid who they just rescued sits on a gurney in the background, ignored by the fans he so desperately craves. The only people who pay attention to him are the other paramedics who all work really hard to not burst into laughter with us.

"So are you going to come down, or what?" Dad ekes the question out between the hiccups that follow his fit of laughter.

"That depends. If a hipster hangs himself on a giant pink balloon and thirty thousand people don't care enough to do anything other than pants him on live television, and the hipster dies, does that count as murder?"

Dad ponders the question for half a second. "Thirty thousand times, yes."

"Well then, save some prison turkey for me. I'll be there in about two hours." I hardly utter the words before there is a knock on the door.

"That should be Inspector Douglas. I told them you were coming to talk about another body."

"How did you know I'd agree to cancel my plans and come see you?" I want to be more irritated with him than I am, but to be honest it's a relief to not have to spend the holiday alone.

"Hen, we took you to SkiBowl when you were eight and you fell down the bunny slope. You managed to fracture your arm in three places before we even put skis on you. You enjoy Mount Hood about as much as you might enjoy getting a root canal."

I nod silently as I hang up the phone. I'm halfway into my coat when I swing the front door open. Standing outside my apartment is a version of Dougy that is more pissed off than a Rottweiler poked with a cattle prod. I try to hide a smirk by turning to lock the door. I don't know if I'm happier because Dad wants to see me today, or that he's pulled Dougy out of his tryptophan coma to play chauffeur.

"Happy Thanksgiving," I chortle.

"This had better be worth missing my mother's famous Boston cream pie." Dougy stomps in his cowboy boots behind me as I walk towards his car. "It seems like every goddamn time she makes that pie, Ollie has some breakthrough."

"Oh?" I turn to look at him.

"I haven't had a slice of her Boston Cream in over fifteen years. She bakes it, your dad contacts me with some issue, and it's always gone by the time I get home."

I laugh so hard, I cry.

## To Do

Valorie pants heavily. The sweat on her body glistens in the dim light that trickles through the slats of the mini-blinds. She's beautiful in the twilight. All of her curves are accentuated and she looks the way that men wish women in magazines really looked. Voluptuous, delicate and with dips and turns in her body soft enough to cup your cock no matter which angle you happen to approach her. I know that I should pay more attention to the perfection of her body but I am fixated on the top drawer of my dresser.

"You look like you're a million miles away." Valorie's voice is as sultry as the night is long. She reaches her hand out to touch my back. "What are you thinking about?"

I look over my shoulder and am greeted by her naked breasts. Her nipples are dark and wide, and in the dim light they are little pieces of chocolate candy begging to be tasted. I know that I should turn around and lick at them. If I did, she would moan and press against me for another round. But instead I shrug an apology. "It's dumb, but I was thinking about my to-do list."

Valorie props herself up on her elbow and

smiles. Her teeth glow and she suddenly takes on the appearance of the Cheshire Cat in Alice and Wonderland. That is, if the Cheshire Cat happened to also haunt the streets of Gotham as Catwoman. "Do you have pressing matters to attend to?"

The smell of sex and heat of arousal rolls off of Valorie in waves. She adjusts her hips and the thick smell of her wetness makes my dick twitch. I turn away from her and look at the dresser again. I've ignored the top drawer for days, but now it calls to me and I can't shut it out. "Yeah. I'm sorry, Valorie, but I've got to get out of here."

Both my sex drive and ego go limp as I feel her crawl around me on the twin sized bed, picking up bits of her clothes from the floor. She pulls each article over her skin as she finds it, never needing to get off the bed. I finally think to put on my pants, but I'm not as practiced at getting dressed in the dark so I get up to turn on the light. When the light floods the room I am presented with a fully clothed woman without a hair out of place. Her rosy cheeks are the only indication that she's exerted herself. And here I am, still naked, my drying limp dick sticking to my left thigh.

Valorie sees my pants before I do. They sit roughly three inches from the place on the bed that still

135

has my ass imprinted on it. She picks them up and tosses them to me. "If they'd been a snake, they'd have bit you."

I almost fall over when I try to pull the pants on while standing. Valorie giggles and smacks me on the bare ass as she passes by to let herself out of my room. By the time I'm upright and trying to zip up without catching my scrotum in the rabid teeth of my zipper, she's already got her coat and boots on.

"I'll call you when I've got some time and maybe we can do this again." The cracks in my voice nullifies any casual inflection that I had intended.

Valorie nods. "I want to do it on the money again."

I smile at her stupidly.

Valorie reaches under her coat and in one motion pulls it, the sweater and blouse she wears up under her chin. She holds her clothes aloft for a moment so I can get one more lengthy view of her cantaloupe sized tits. "And I want you to come on these."

I fight the throb of my groin. I turn sideways as we hug so that my half-erect cock doesn't accidentally brush against her. All I can think to say in response to her offer is, "I'll call you soon."

As soon as I make sure Valorie's breasts are once again secured under her clothes I usher her out of the apartment and lock the door. As I trot back down the hallway to my bedroom, my dick finishes peeling itself off my thigh and wrestles against the thick denim of my pants. I reach the dresser and pull the top drawer open.

My hands dive into the drawer. They search and grope through rolled up socks the way they should be groping between Valorie's thighs. My fingers brush the list and I read the next item on the page. *Buy an assortment of prizes worth winning.*

I've spent the last week buying up more Visa and MasterCard prepaid cards. I've picked up a few hundred dollar's worth every time I stop into the store for something. Every single checker comments about how lucky my family is to be to getting all that money for Christmas.

"It's time to go to the store." I lay the list down on my bed and loosen my pants. I fantasize about all of the things I'm going to buy. I'll have to get some video game consoles and skateboards for the kids. But there's got to be some prizes for adults, too.

What if an attractive woman wins the contest? Maybe she could win some sexy lingerie. Maybe she'd be so excited to win a contest that she'd want to try it on right then and there. She could be any kind of woman, but maybe she'd be a woman like Valorie.

My fantasy fades and the grasp I've got on my throbbing groin loosens. I shake my head in disgust as I realize that I could be screwing Valorie right now instead of rubbing one out to a fantasy on a piece of paper. If I bought Valorie lingerie, I know she'd wear it for me. She'd prance around in it for a while before giving me permission to tear it off of her. I feel stupid and wonder why I do this to myself. I don't understand what's going on. Nobody could possibly understand.

… except Jeanne. What if Jeanne wins my contest? I certainly wouldn't want her to feel gypped out of an amazing prize. No, for Jeanne I'd want to make sure she walked away with a pair of new stockings and a set of old fashioned garters to hold them in place. A tight black thong to show off her ass, and a corset to accentuate her hourglass waistline. She'd want to make sure the corset fit before she took it home, and I could help her lace it up.

I lay my face down on the bed next to my list. My breath is ragged and each exhale makes the paper crackle. I imagine Jeanne in front of me, my fingers entwined in the laces of her corset. When I pull them tight, her body falls against me and my dick thrusts between her thighs. Her damp panties rub against the head and she begs me to push inside of her. I let go of the corset laces and it falls between us. I pull her panties away from her cunt. It's hot and tight when I push my fingers inside of her and she moans.

I come against the side of my bed and cry out for Jeanne. My orgasm is fierce and seems to last an eternity. My vision blurs and I'm able to hold onto the fantasy a moment longer. I am with her and she loves me. She wants to fuck me. She wants to help me.

My eyes snap open against the darkness and I realize that today I missed my therapy appointment.

# Reschedule

I'm at Jeanne's office at seven forty-five even though I know the receptionist won't unlock the front door until eight. There  is a smattering of cars in the parking lot and I entertain myself by trying to guess which one is Jeanne's. I settle on a riced out Mini Cooper that has flashy paint and a giant set of pink fuzzy dice hanging from the rear view mirror. The spoiler stands taller than it should, and the fenders flare to accentuate the small car's curves. It would be just like Jeanne to have a car that is flashy but sensible on the budget.

The clock on my dashboard ticks away until the minute hand passes the top of the hour. It's three minutes after when I see the mousey receptionist turn the lock in the glass double doors and try the handle to make sure the door swings freely when it's pushed. Despite my normal penchant for names, I have to concentrate to remember hers. I'm pretty sure she's a Cheryl or Sherry.

I wait for her to turn back to her desk before I get out of my car. She sits at her computer and is already typing away on her Facebook page by the time I reach her desk. She is pretty in a generic office worker kind of way. I steal a look at her post before she notices me. She's posting a picture of a beautiful casserole dish that was obviously cooked by someone else and photographed in a studio to make it look more edible than it really is. I've never understood women's desire to share such ordinary fantasies on social media. Whenever I get the urge to check out a woman's profile online, all I usually find are recipes she'll never make, projects she'll never start and dream homes she'll never own.

"Hello, Mr. Wilson. Can I help you?"

"Hey, Cher." I wait for her to tell me that isn't her name, but she just stares at me in anticipation. "I had an appointment yesterday with Jeanne and I totally spaced it."

"Mmhmmm. Are you wanting to reschedule?" Her finger reaches for the enter key and she finishes submitting her generic Facebook post.

"If it wouldn't be too much trouble. I know Jeanne keeps a strict schedule and I feel bad for messing it up."

Cheryl / Sherry nods absently and starts to type. I find myself going on a long and detailed description of how sorry I am that I missed my appointment. I tell her it's never happened before, and I hope it will never

141

happen again.

"She has a slot open at four o' clock today, if you're available then." She looks up over the counter at me with a sly look. "We keep that time open for delinquents like you."

I'm glad that I am coherent enough to understand she's joking. What if I were a little crazier, though? It seems like the kind of joke that you shouldn't throw out around mentally deficient people. "That's fine. I'll be back then."

I head to the car. I get behind the wheel and turn the engine over. I've got eight hours to fill before I get to see Jeanne and I may as well make them productive. I head towards the river, doing my best to not get pissed at the congestion piled up along Sandy Boulevard. Despite the assholes who can't figure out how to drive in the foggy drizzle, I find myself at the Office Depot on MLK in just a few minutes.

I grab a stack of bills from my glove compartment and pull a baseball cap out of the back seat. I slap myself in the face to shock my nerves. I'm not doing anything wrong. I just need to pick up some supplies. I pull the hat on low over my face and shove the cash in my pocket.

A beefy guy approaches me as I wander down

the cell phone aisle. "Hey there. Can I help you?"

I cast a sideways glance at him and shrug my shoulders. He moves toward me with more confidence than I've had in my entire life. His khaki pants and polo shirt are adorned with a crooked white name tag with the letters worn off. His uniform is so universal that he could work at any of the big box stores in Portland. I bet when he goes to Target or Fred Meyer on his way home from work people assume he works there, too.

"I need a phone."

I think the sales guy smiles at me, but it's hard to tell under his sculpted mustache. For the life of me I don't know why men today are obsessed with over the top facial hair, although standing next to this guy's carefully coiffed lip hair I can almost taste the testosterone that pours off of him.

"Well, you've got a lot of options. What kind of setup do you need?" Sales guy leans casually against the shelf and drags his fingers over the keys of a sleek silver model.

"I'm not sure, really. Something that I can just pay cash for, I guess."

"We've got lots of prepaid phone options these days. Carriers have finally picked up that people don't want the hassle of a contract. Now you can get phones

143

with texting, data, all of the stuff you're used to with your smart phone but without a two year commitment. Here, take a look at this guy." He hands me the cell phone he's been molesting. I don't take it.

"I don't really need all of that. I just want to have a phone number that someone can call."

The mustache quivers, and a twinkle gleams in his eye. "Ah. You want something discreet?"

I nod, unsure of what to say.

"Hey, I've been there. It's hard to keep a little someone on the side when that little someone keeps calling your cell phone. Then you've got to explain to your wife who this new phone number on the bill belongs to, and it's only a matter of time before she figures out that 'Stan from work' is really 'Stacy from Hooters' and everything goes tits up." The mustache falls momentarily and he puts his hand on my shoulder for support.

"Bitches." I shrug.

The mustache rolls along his cheeks when he laughs. "I know, right? Let's get you set up, man. What you want is something basic that you can carry and drop. Look at this guy here." He moves toward the far end of the aisle and tosses me a little black phone the size of a deck of cards. "It's got a slide-out keyboard in

144

case you decide you want to text, and has a decent track pad for getting into your menu to clear your history under pressure. Best of all, you just come in to any Office Depot and buy one of these minute cards to load it when you need to. No pesky statements or anything."

"And when I'm done with it, I can just throw it away?" The phone is light in my hands, made of a cheap plastic and I worry it will crack if I squeeze it too hard.

Mustache gets very serious with me. He was lighthearted when talking about adultery, but now he looks as if he might hit me. "It's plastic, man. Recycle."

"Right. Of course. And the phone number will stay the same?"

"As long as you keep it loaded with minutes, the number is yours." The mustache settles down again and curls into a smile.

"I'll take it."

I check out and the guy helps me to activate the phone. Without my asking, he makes up a false address, name and birth date for the activation. "That way if your wife finds the phone, you can say you found it on the sidewalk and when she calls the company, the information seems legit," he explains.

We shake hands as we part ways. He seems

145

happy to be partners in conspiracy, but he doesn't know the depth of how he's helped me. When I go through with my plan, this guy will have blood on his hands without realizing it. Dad always tells me that most men are stupid and I'm starting to believe him.

I pull my regular cell phone out of my pocket and do a Google search to see if there are any payphones left in Portland. I find one just up the road at a car wash and head over to test out the prepaid phone. When I get there, I'm greeted with a booth filled with the filth of a thousand unwashed hands. The whole thing is in rough shape and I count myself lucky that the receiver is still attached to the box. I'm not willing to touch it though, and decide it will be good enough just to call the line and see if it rings. I get close enough to make out the number on the phone's label and dial. Half a second later the payphone springs to life, screaming out at the world that someone remembers it exists.

I let the rings peal out into the cold air a dozen times before I hang up. The payphone falls silent on its hook, once again a forgotten fixture useful only to kids hanging up band posters, illicit women leaving calling cards, and low income families looking for a place to post lost kitten ads. The cord is limp, the handset cold

146

and dead in its cradle.

I know just how it feels.

# Office Space

At three thirty I once again sit in the parking lot of Jeanne's office. I don't want to seem paranoid about being on time for my appointment so I park in the far corner of the lot where I can't be seen from the receptionist's desk. I thumb through the menu on the disposable phone to kill time, but there simply isn't much in there. I'm not entering any contacts into it, and I don't have any desire to play solitaire on a two inch screen.

I lean back in my seat and close my eyes for a minute. I haven't been sleeping particularly well. Dougy wants to take Dad on another field trip and insists that I need to tag along. Dad said we'd be heading to a place with naked women to look at. There are a thousand strip clubs, peep shows and adult super centers in Portland. I know that I am a pretty messed up individual, but even I don't want to have a stripper grind on me while my father looks on.

A wild vibration against my thigh startles me. Aerosmith's "Come Together" blares at me from my front pocket, and I thrash around the front seat as I try to dig my phone out. I think I find it, but the prepaid phone appears in my hand instead. I toss it in a cup holder and fish my real phone out, answering it just before it goes to voice mail.

"An inmate is attempting to reach you from the Sheridan Federal Correctional Institute. Please press the star key to accept the charges."

I hit the button on my phone, but the line sounds dead. "Hello?"

"Henry." The voice on the other end of the line is foreign.

"Who is this?" I do my best to not sound panicked but secretly I'm worried that something has happened to Dad and this disembodied voice has raided his cell and found my number.

"I'm a friend of Ollie's. I am calling to tell you that we know what you're doing, and no matter what happens we will have your back." The line clicks, there is a low hiss like a deflating tire and then my phone beeps to signal the call's end.

I look down at my cell phone's screen just as it goes dark. The smart phone powers itself off and I rattle it around in my hands for a couple of seconds to try and figure out what's going on. The battery is intact, nothing looks broken, and when I hit the power button it boots right up.

I glance at the corner of the screen and

suddenly realize that its five minutes to four. I forget the creepy phone call and drop my cell back into my pocket. I lock the prepaid phone in my glove box with the cash left over from my errand running and jump out of the car, locking it behind me.

The forgettable receptionist peeks over her desk at me as I push the door open. The lobby is empty aside from two mid-eighties office chairs and a plant that is getting baked in the afternoon sun.

"You made it."

I nod as I sign in the guest log on the desk corner and take a seat next to the dying plant. Jeanne opens her office door just as I start to peel the brown edges off of the crumbling leaves beside me. Her smile is bright and I feel my chest swell at the sight of her.

"I'm so sorry that I missed our appointment yesterday." I stand up and walk toward Jeanne as I apologize.

"No worries," she replies with a wry grin. "It just meant I had an extra hour to nap."

We chuckle together as we move into her office and get comfortable in our respective chairs. She pushes the box of tissues to the back corner of the table. I'm glad that we both feel as though the days of tears and nose-blowing are behind us.

"Does it happen very often?" I notice the confusion as it spreads across Jeanne's face and I stammer, "Getting stood up for appointments."

"It happens here and there." Jeanne sets her pen and paper beside her. Poised for note-taking should anything interesting come up. "Truthfully, I leave the four o' clock appointment slot open in case there are emergencies that need to be tended to. Whenever someone is in crisis, I want them to know that I always have time for them."

I beam at how considerate she is. "Well, I'm not in crisis. But I'm glad that I was able to get in to see you anyway."

"I'm glad to see you, too." Jeanne uncrosses her legs and leans forward in her chair. A wisp of hair falls across her forehead. It makes her look younger and more vulnerable than she probably is.

"I've been seeing someone." The statement is abrupt and awkward. It wasn't really what I was hoping to lead our session with but now the confession floats in the air around us, sucking the air out of the room.

"Oh?" Pen to paper. "Tell me about her."

"Her name is Valorie. She's pretty, and smells nice." I wring my hands. My mind has gone blank and now I can't remember anything about Valorie. Jeanne's curled lashes and dimpled smile push Valorie out of my mind. I can't remember what she looks like or how she sounds when she calls my name in the dark passion of sex. All I know is Jeanne's wrist flicks slightly as she writes and I long to feel the tips of her fingers caress my lips.

"How did you meet?" Jeanne pierces me with her eyes and I am filled with regret for ever meeting another woman.

"She works at my bank. She helped me one day." I stare down at the carpet between us. It's worn in funny places as if it used to be home to different furniture with wider legs.

"You certainly are good at meeting people. Do you consider yourself to be an extrovert?" Jeanne smiles warmly, as if all is forgiven. She understands that I don't mean to be with other women. Maybe it's just the way I am. Monogamy just another tick on the long list of things that I can't do.

"I've never really thought about it. I don't really like talking to other people, but I guess when they're in front of me I push past that."

"That's a really useful skill to have." Jeanne writes, nods and compliments in one graceful motion. "A lot of adults never learn to push through their shyness. I'm sure that ability serves you well in your work and personal relationships."

"I suppose so." The air clears around us and I find the ability to breathe again.

Jeanne sets her pen down and folds her hands in her lap casually. "So what's new? What have you been up to this week?"

"Well, I'm working on a big project and I'm making some headway."

"Taxidermy?" This time Jeanne doesn't even have to look at her notes. She just remembers that detail of my life off the cuff, and I fall in love with her all over again.

"Yes. Well, the prep work for the taxidermy anyway." I search for a way to put my cereal contest in to taxidermist terms. I falter for a moment but then the story clicks. "I'm setting up a shop of my own. Well, my dad will help me, of course. But overall it will be mine."

"That's good to hear." Jeanne reaches over and scrawls a quick note, but I don't mind.

"Yeah, it will be great. I just signed up for our business phone today." Buying a phone for the purpose of finding someone to murder suddenly feels lighter. It's not murder, it's just a business transaction.

153

"What's it called?" Jeanne's smile goes a little wider with excitement but I feel my face fall.

"What's what called?"

Jeanne's laugh rings through the office. "Your taxidermy shop. What are you calling yourselves?"

"I hadn't thought about a name."

Jeanne chuckles some more, and soon the pink in her cheeks turns a darker shade of red. I laugh along with her. The happiness of the moment makes me dizzy and I hold onto the arms of my chair for balance. I'm not sure if it's been seconds or hours when our giggles subside.

"When I started my therapy practice, I had the name picked out before I even knew what city I might live in."

I'm touched by this personal bit of information from Jeanne. She doesn't talk about herself much, which I suppose makes her a great therapist. It makes it hard for me to pinpoint what it is I love about her sometimes, though. I grin as I imagine a younger version of Jeanne walking out of her college dorm holding the sign that now hangs in front of her office.

"Just how long did it take you to come up with the name 'Men's Resource Center'? I bet you spent a lot of sleepless nights before settling on that one." I wink

154

at Jeanne and she bursts into laughter again.

"You must be feeling better. You're on fire today, Peter." Jeanne wipes a tear from her eye. She sits up straight again and tries to look more professional than the moment calls for. "Lets assign you the homework of coming up with a name. I look forward to hearing more about that."

I lean back in my chair and think about what I'll need for my cereal contest that I might also need if I were starting a taxidermy business. It suddenly occurs to me that either way, I wouldn't want people coming to meet me at my apartment. "I really need to find a business space."

"How much space?" Jeanne starts to write a list on her pad of paper. She wants to remember this conversation so that she can ask me about my progress next week. She is so good at keeping me on task with all of my goals. She's better than a casual girlfriend because she always follows up and holds me accountable for the things I say I'll do. I wonder if she'll do that when we're married?

The daydream I'm in snaps closed. The fog lifts and I remember that we are having an actual conversation and I'd better respond. "I'm not sure. I can do most of it out of my apartment, you know. But I need a place to meet customers and set up a more professional display. Can't really show off a thirteen foot grizzly with eight foot ceilings."

Jeanne's eyes dart towards me. "Grizzly bears grow to be thirteen feet tall?"

I shrug. The bear we found Sasha in was close to ten feet tall, and Dad had said that it wasn't fully matured. "I have no idea. But it sounded good."

Jeanne leans over the edge of her chair and opens a drawer on the side of her table. Hanging file folders swing toward her on metal rails and her fingers dance across the file tabs. "If all you need is a place to meet clients, I may be able to help you. There is a company that contacts me every so often to see if they can lease out our conference room. They set up temporary conference spaces for small business people. You can rent a space for an hour or an afternoon, and they've got spots all over the city."

She nods as she finds the file she's looking for and pulls a business card out. I reach forward and she presses it into my hand gently. "It might be just what you need. You could make an appointment, get there an hour before to set up your displays, and then at the end of the meeting break it all down and keep it in storage."

"Jeanne, this is exactly what I needed. Thank

you."

## Fantasy

There are so many cars parked in the bottleneck on Southwest Coronado Street that I have to park at the bottom of the hill and hike up to Fantasy for Adults Only. I've been here a half dozen times and have never seen more than three cars parked in the lot. Granted, every other time I've come it has been when I suddenly realize that my porn collection needs to be beefed up. That doesn't typically happen during peak shopping hours.

The video store employees huddle outside of the crime scene tape. The manager is a tall, sinewy man who is too clean cut to be straight. He tries to invoke the spirit of the brutish high school quarterback he used to be as he shouts at the police officer in charge of keeping them off the property. The pale pink gloss that glistens off of his manicured fingernails and perfectly arched penciled on eyebrows make him just femme enough to not be taken seriously. He's surrounded by a staff of misfit girls, all gorgeous in their own nonconformist way. They crowd together under half length coats and shredded jeans, dressed for a shift in a hundred degree showroom under fluorescent display lights instead of the twenty-four degree winter day they stand in.

I duck under the tape right in front of them, close enough to the manager that his arm brushes my goose down coat when I pass by. Watching me saunter onto the lot they've been exiled from breathes new fire in his declarations of injustice and I hear him threaten to sue the city. I don't think he knows how criminal investigations work.

Dad stands in the middle of the parking lot, gleefully watching the chaos as it ebbs and flows around him. A combination of city police and Search and Rescue volunteers move in hurried fits around the parking lot as they try to stay warm while they wait for orders. I wonder why none of them think to go sit in their cars with the heat on while they wait, but the grin on Dad's face tells me that he demanded they be out there with him. Dougy is on the far end of the lot and I head toward him.

"Hey." My breath comes out in a fog through the zipper of my upturned collar. "Sorry for being late. I didn't realize everyone was waiting on me."

Dougy wears no less than three coats. He is so tightly packed into the third one that he can't get the zipper shut, making him look more obese than he actually is. "Ollie won't start without you, but every

159

time someone goes to find a heater he starts pretending he's ready for us to search."

My coat collar keeps my smile covered. I look over at Dad in his windbreaker and orange jumpsuit. He gives me a long wink. Dougy sees the gesture.

"Your dad is a fucking asshole." Dougy pulls at his first and second collars and spits over them onto the pavement. The glob of saliva immediately takes on the sheen of newly forming ice. He looks at me and adds, "No offense."

"None taken." I look around to see that everyone has come in closer, hoping to get the search over so that they can go home. I jog over to Dad. "You about ready?"

"So good to see you, Son." Dad lifts his handcuffed hands over my head and down my back in a prison style bear-hug that feels more tender than it looks. "Of course I'm ready. Are you?"

I nod. "I'm working things out with my plan. Everything is moving a few steps forward, so far no steps back."

"Good. Now let me tell you a story about selling taxidermy cast-offs for profit." Dad releases me and walks toward the front door of the store. I follow him, and about fifteen shivering people follow me. "At

160

the height of my hobby, I had a lot of spare parts to offload. Skeletons, mostly. Most of them were complete so I cleaned, assembled and sold them to collectors. But a fair portion of the time I ended up with partial remains and pieces that were too damaged to display."

Dad stops on the sidewalk and takes a seat on the curb. I settle down next to him, doing my best to ignore the searing cold that jumps from the cement through my jeans and into to my ass. Everyone else hovers just out of earshot, trying to stay far enough away to keep Dad talking.

"I held onto those spare bits for a long time. The dump doesn't take them, and there's just so many coyotes that a man can bury in his own back yard, you know? Then one night I'm here talking to the manager." Dad squints as he looks beyond the yellow tape blowing in the wind. He points to the current manager who has stopped yelling at the officers and is now snuggled together with the five girls under a lap blanket that someone must have had in their car. "It wasn't that guy. Back then this place was run by a man with different tastes."

I blink hard. The corners of my eyes ache with the effort. "Christ, Dad. You didn't supply a necrophiliac with love slaves, did you?"

"Shit, Son. No." Dad shoves his hands deeper in his pockets. "What kind of psycho do you think I am?" I look at him long and hard. He shrugs noncommittally, then turns my disapproving look back on me. "How many times do I have to tell you that Christ doesn't approve of us using his name that way?"

"Sorry, Dad." My muttered apology gets lost in the down of my jacket.

"As I was saying." Dad looks up at a volunteer who has come too close for comfort. When their eyes meet, the cherub faced woman's eyes go wide and she scurries back a few feet. "The manager here had a taste for oddities, and he had a legitimate landscape concern. He wanted to spruce the lot up a bit so the locals would feel this place was more high end so we worked out a deal for him to use my cast-offs as gravel filler."

I look around at the thickets of ivy that grow all around us. Even in the bitter cold, the plants are green and thick around the base of the trees. Most places you can't even see dirt and it looks as if the ivy shoots straight up out of the pavement. Where there isn't ivy, there are evergreen bushes growing in clumps six feet high and twelve feet across. There isn't a piece of gravel in sight.

"What kind of bones are we talking about here, Dad?"

"Vertebrae, mostly. But a few knuckles and knee caps may have made it in as well. Just kind of depended on what I had on hand at the time. There was a while there where I was processing a lot of deer and moose. Man, moose vertebrae are something else altogether. Big and bulky. He loved them, though. They really stood out in the mix." Dad spreads his hand out and I can tell he can see the image of a giant backbone in his palm.

"How many bones did you sell him?" I keep hoping that Dad will just tell me who we're actually up here to discover. I know he's going to make me keep talking about it though so that he can savor both the opportunity to impart wisdom on me and enjoy some time out in the fresh air.

"A hundred buckets full. Or more. It took several months, of course. But little by little I'd bring them up here and he'd pay me twenty bucks a bucket for them." Dad looks at me as if he's just scratched the winning numbers off of a lotto ticket. "Can you imagine? Twenty bucks just for stuff I had laying around."

I do my best to suppress an eye roll. A normal

163

father might tell this same story, but he'd be talking about selling buckets of scrap nails. Or vinyl records. I don't think my dad will ever understand that it's not normal to have five gallon buckets full of bones just "laying around".

Dad notices me stiffen up. He pulls a hand out of his jacket pocket and pats me on the back. "Anyway. That was years ago. Look around now." He glares at the current manager with daggers in his eyes. "That guy has let this place go to shit."

I can't hold my sigh back. "It's a jack-off store, Dad. People don't come here for the landscape."

He plugs one nostril and blows a wad of snot out of the other. It must be a trick he picked up in prison because I've never seen him do anything so disgusting before. He grunts. "Well, it wouldn't hurt to put a little effort into it."

Dougy materializes in front of us. He is so close that our shoes touch. I'd pull mine back, but I don't want him to feel he has the upper hand. I pretend to cross my legs and kick him in the shin. He glares at me and Dad cackles.

"Well?" Dougy's hands are placed where I imagine his hips might be. It's hard to tell under all of his layers, especially since he isn't really gifted in the hip department to begin with.

"Dad sold the manager a bunch of bones left over from taxidermy projects. The guy used them as gravel in the landscape." I watch Dougy eye the imposing bushes the same way I had just a minute before.

"How many?" Dougy crouches in front of us. His breath smells as if his last meal was made up of rubbing alcohol and sausage.

"He says a hundred buckets full." I look at Dad. "Right?"

"Or more." He sees Dougy's face go red from squatting and decides to help him out before he has a hernia from being this low to the ground. "They weren't all human though, Inspector Douglas. I promise."

"How many people, Ollie?" Dougy and Dad lean together as if they are old friends. For a minute it seems that they might clasp hands and embrace like reunited frat brothers at a forty year class reunion. The moment is fleeting, and soon Dougy again looks like he wants to go home.

"It's hard to say, really. It was toward the end of things and I had kept a lot of bits and pieces." Dad averts his gaze from me now, as if he's embarrassed for me to know this particular detail. "If I had to take a

165

guess, it would probably be fifteen to twenty individuals. Mostly male. Mostly gay."

I look at Dad and he looks right though me, back over the yellow caution tape at the flamboyant manager. A cloud of white steam jets into the air as if the breath is knocked out of him. He seems to shrink beside me, a man who has failed his purpose and who will never be given a second chance. "You can't save everyone," he whispers.

Dougy's knees pop when he stands up. He takes a moment to flex his joints, then turns on his heel and barks out orders. "Everybody grab a bucket and a shovel from the SAR truck, then fan out and start digging. Pull up every plant, bush or weed and dig down six to twelve inches until you get below the bark dust. We're looking for anything that might be a bone. Even if you aren't sure it's human, pull it and we'll sort through it later. If the ground is too frozen to dig, we'll tape everything off and come back when the winds change."

I put my hand on Dad's knee. He pushes against my shoulder with his own and we sit there for a while. It starts to snow and I look up into the clouds above us. I block out all of the other people and for a moment I am just a boy, he is just my Dad, and we are just sitting on the curb together watching the winter snow.

# Christmas Shopping

I stand in front of the Toys 'R Us store and count the Visa gift cards I've got in my hand. I've decided to use half of them as prizes because there's never a time when people don't want to win money. All told, I've bought nearly three thousand dollars worth of prepaid cards and that means that I've got fifteen hundred bucks burning a hole in my pocket.

I follow throngs of parents into the store but I don't share their tense body language or curt mannerisms. A guy walking beside me lets out a string of profanity as he tries to make out the writing on the Christmas list in his hands. His genius kid wrote it in yellow crayon on a yellow legal pad. I'm instantly glad that I don't have anyone at home to be disappointed if I don't come home with the right animatronic Elmo.

I grab one of the few unclaimed carts and enter the store. I've decided I'm going to buy every toy that I ever wished I could have had as a kid. I'm surprised when fifty Furbys greet me from a display case just inside the entrance. I consider them for a minute, then pick out one green and one purple. Mom had said Furbys were the devil. She insisted that their only real function was to record people's every move and memorize bank account numbers. The sensitive information would then be repeated after parents forgot about the Furby's memory capacity, donating them to Goodwill to later be purchased by bored housewives who weren't afraid of credit card fraud charges. Maybe that's all they were. But if she'd bought me one before she died then maybe I would have had something to talk to all these years without her.

I drop superheroes, building blocks, and a couple of gaming consoles into my cart. I'm amazed at how quickly it fills up and in less than an hour it overflows with planes, trains and automobiles. I don't want to be sexist, so I toss a few dolls on the heap for good measure and head toward the registers.

There are a dozen check stands open and people are gathered around them like a swarm of angry bees. A cacophony of beeps, buzzers and shouts fills the air. I try to choose a lane but no one is standing in any kind of organized line. As I steel myself for the task of pushing through the crowd someone touches my arm. The sensation makes me jump and I spin around to look at my assailant.

A short, fat teenager throws a smile at me that's filled with glittering braces and enthusiasm. "I can take care of you at the Customer Service desk."

I follow him as he waddles around the boom of pissed off parents who waited too late in the shopping season. He unconsciously shakes his right leg every time his slacks ride up in his butt crack. I duck behind the pile of toys I'm pushing until I can only see the top of the curly mop on his head to keep from laughing.

In contrast to the craziness that surrounds the registers, Customer Service is a desolate wasteland. Everyone is buying and no one is returning. In a few weeks when all the kiddies open their presents and complain that Santa brought them the red haired doll when what they wanted was a blonde, the tide will reverse. I doubt that the pimple faced kid helping me today will be quite so eager then.

"You've got a lot of loot." His voice doesn't so much crack as it skitters through the octaves. He grabs the dolls at the top of the stack and starts scanning barcodes.

"I guess so. I've got a lot of kids to shop for." I pat the square in my pocket where the Visa cards sit, trying to imagine the people who will actually take these toys home, oblivious to the brush with death that they will experience. I shudder at myself.

"Are you one of those Mormons or something?" The kid doesn't skip a beat in his methodical scanning as he talks.

"No. I'm some kind of Christian, I guess. I don't go to church." I wonder what Dad would have said to me if we had met on the street and I had admitted that. Would he have decided I had enough faith to go on living? Or am I the kind of guy he'd invite over for a home cooked meal and a turn filling up a bucket for the Fantasy store on the hill?

"Just wondering. I've been watching that Sister Wives show on Netflix. I'd love to have that many women lined up for me every night, but damn. That's a lot of kids." The teenager's neck rolls clap together softly as he shakes his head.

"I've never seen it."

"You should watch it." The kid looks at me seriously as he pushes a lawnmower that blows bubbles over the counter. "I'm thinking about converting."

We're silent as he dredges through the last dozen toys in the bottom of my cart. When he's done, my total flashes up on the register and I hand him the wad of plastic cards for payment. Despite the fact that I haven't kept track of the cost of the toys as they entered my basket, I've finished with a fifty dollar visa left over. The kid hands me the unused card, a couple of dollars in change, and my yardstick of a receipt.

171

I hand the gift card back to him. "You know what? Keep this one."

The sweat glistens on his cheeks from the effort of unloading, scanning and reloading my cart. "For realsies?"

"For realsies. Merry Christmas."

# Comic Sans

I boot up the laptop I found at the Goodwill on 185th at a corner table in Starbucks. I've bought my obligatory coffee and am using it to hold down the scrap of paper that holds the WIP key for the Wi-Fi. When the desktop is live, I enter the Wi-Fi password and open up a web browser. Immediately I am greeted with auto loaded Pinterest, Instagram and Pandora tabs. All of them signed in.

Miranda Wood has a station dedicated to the song "Fergalicious". She is followed by ten thousand Instagram followers who are currently engaged in a photo of the new luggage that she purchased for a trip to see her parents in Miami for Christmas. She's also pinned the same casserole recipe that Jeanne's receptionist posted to her Facebook page earlier in the week. "Birds of a feather," I mumble.

I minimize Miranda's stupidity, but don't bother to log out of any of it. She's lucky that I'm not the kind of person interested in stealing her identity. Especially if she's got all of her bank accounts set to automatically sign in as well, and I suspect she has. Instead, I open a new browser tab and hunt around online until I find a free template that matches the two hundred labels sitting in my backpack. I play around with the twelve available fonts and some wording until I'm pleased with the result.

Congratulations, you may have won!
$1,000,000 in cash and prizes.
Call now!

I consider whether or not I can get away with saying I have a million dollars in prizes. I decide that in this murderous venture I have bigger things to worry about than false advertising claims. I finish the labels out by adding the disposable cell phone number.

"Can I get you anything else?" The Starbucks is slow at the moment and the baristas have floated away from the espresso machines to clean up from the last swarm of caffeine addicts. The one talking to me is lanky, blonde and looks like she'd be more at home on a yacht than in a green apron wiping down tables.

"Do you guys have a printer I can use?"

She pushes her ponytail over he shoulder. "We aren't supposed to let customers use it."

I reach across the aisle between us and place my hand over hers. The damp towel makes her skin cool. "I promise to buy fifteen more coffees and give

174

you a twenty dollar tip."

Her ponytail drops down in  front of her shoulder again and she smiles at me. "Make it twenty five so I can afford a pedicure, and you've got a deal."

We wrestle the odd-sized sticker sheets into their back office printer. I click the print button on the laptop and the machine sets to work. Sammi the barista heads back to the front of the cafe to start brewing my tower of coffee, leaving me alone in the manager's office. I glance down at the safe under the desk and wonder at how much she trusts me. The first row of stickers plops out of the printer into the tray. The pages are coming out a little crooked, so I adjust the feed and wait.

A half hour later I hold two hundred golden labels, have cleared the sticker template from the web history and re-donated the laptop back to Goodwill. I head toward my apartment with five cup holders full of black coffee lining the floorboards in my backseat. I pull into a Park and Ride lot and park near the platform.

I shout out at the people waiting for the train. "Free coffee!"

Everyone looks at me with suspicion until they notice the Starbucks logo on the sides of the cups. In minutes I've given away the whole lot, randomly

175

wishing them a Merry Christmas or Happy Hanukkah. A couple of stragglers approach me, but when they see that my hands are empty they trudge back to the platform in disappointment.

I pull my phone out of my pocket and scroll through my history until I see Valorie's number. I hit talk and listen for the click of her picking up the phone. "Hey. You want to meet up after work?"

"I'm off in an hour." Her voice is clipped and professional. She's supposed to strictly enforce the policy of no personal calls at work so she pretends I'm a loan officer from another bank. "Can you get me the docs before then?"

"Sure," I say. "The dick will be ready when you arrive."

She stifles a laugh and the line goes dead.

## Print on Demand

I decide that my whole scheme will look more legitimate if I have a badge declaring that I am a representative of Alphabet Apes. I drive to a FedEx Office Print Center that is as far across my GPS map as I'm willing to drive. Banners hanging in the windows advertise custom printed holiday cards, party invitations and decorative posters.

The store is split into two sections; one side for printing, the other for shipping. The shipping area is bombarded with people who frantically seek assurance that their packages will reach their destinations before Christmas. The print side is empty aside from a bored woman who cuts split ends out of the length of her hair with industrial cardboard shears.

"Welcome to FedEx, your personal print center. How can I help?" The woman doesn't look up at me as she speaks. The scissor blades dance dangerously close to her fingers and I wince as she snaps them shut, trimming away a millimeter of her hair.

"I need to get a name badge and some business cards printed, please." I fish a flash dive out of my pocket and drop it on the counter in front of her.

"No Christmas cards?" When I shake my head

she hops down from her stool and drops the scissors into a pen holder. "Thank God. If I have to arrange one more card full of people in matching holiday sweaters, I think I might kill myself."

"I don't even own a holiday sweater." I force a grin and point to the gray hooded sweatshirt I'm wearing.

"Me either. So, a name badge and business cards. Easy enough. You have a layout on your drive?" She picks up the stick drive and plugs it into her USB port.

"I do for the badge, but not for the business cards. They just need to be white with black text. A logo if you can fit it."

The print girl nods and fills out a form. She asks me questions about lamination, embossing and whether or not I need to buy a lanyard. Each box that she ticks on the screen gets me one step closer to where I want to be. She prints a proof for me to take a look at of both the business cards and the badge. I sign off on them and then turn to leave.

"Hey," she calls after me. She pulls the false name I gave her off the form. "Ted, I know that our guarantee is to have your documents printed in four hours but as you can see, I've got a serious lack of shit to do today. Do you want to just sit and wait? This is only going to take me twenty minutes."

"Sure." I turn back toward the counter and FedEx girl gestures to a metal stool beside her.

"Have a seat. Just look professional if someone comes to talk to you. Ask them to wait and then come get me." I nod and she hits a few keystrokes on the computer to start the print job and lock her terminal. I watch the other customers jockey for position at the shipping table for a bit, and suddenly she's back at my side with a laminated badge and fifty business cards. "So what do you do for this Alphabet Apes cereal company, anyway?"

I busy myself with pulling out some cash to pay for the job so that I don't have to look her in the eye. "Market research, mostly. Checking out the local demographic for the home office." I gesture at the small bundle of cards. "I lost all of my stuff on the plane ride in. I've got to be out in the field tomorrow and just couldn't wait for the airline to find my luggage."

"Shit, I hate when that happens." FedEx girl offers me a receipt, but I wave it off so she chucks it in the trash.

"Yeah, me too. But thanks for getting me taken

care of so quickly. You're a real life saver." I give her as confident of a smile as I can muster, only slightly

conflicted in the knowledge that she's not saving anybody.

# Restock

For the last several weeks I've been buying groceries around town at odd hours to pick the store I'll use for my test. I've settled on a giant 24 hour store in a suburb west of the city that stocks its shelves overnight. In addition to grocery store employees, food manufacturers send their own employees in to check sale displays and deliver product. I've come to this Winco Foods every night for the last week to chat up the employees and casually walk the aisles as I shop. Tonight, I see the Alphabet Apes company truck parked behind the grocery store. I park next to it and climb up on the delivery ramp to let myself in the back.

I learned a long time ago that the easiest way to blend in is to just act as if you belong. It was something that the Cowlitz County CASA director told me when I was fifteen, transferred to a Washington foster home because I'd been rejected out of so many homes in the Oregon system. "Just pretend you've lived there your whole life and the people around you are the new ones," she'd said. "If you act like you have all the answers, no one will know any different."

I pull the badge from FedEx out of my pocket and loop the lanyard around my neck. The plastic ID slaps against my chest when I walk. I grab a clipboard off of a nearby shelf and follow the aisles until I'm deposited into the bulk foods section at the back of the store. I cut through the barrels of loose pasta and organic rice and stop in front of a pallet stacked six feet high with unopened cases of cereal.

A fit young man in jeans and a t-shirt opens the cases by hand. He punches the taped seam at the top, causing the tape to snap open, then rips the flaps apart. In one fluid motion he spins the box on its head, lifts the cardboard and exposes twelve new boxes of cereal on the pallet. He tosses the empty cardboard shell to the side, picks up the whole stack of cereal in his arms and deposits it on the shelf with the practiced repetition of a precision machine.

"Excuse me."

The man doesn't look at me. He simply grabs another box off the shelf, marks it off of the list beside him, punches the top of the box and proceeds to rip, dump and shelve the cereal. I notice that he's wearing earbuds and an iPod shifts in his pocket as he moves. He hasn't even heard me. His name tag flashes by, and it faces me just long enough to read it.

"Hey, Andrew!" I beam enthusiastically and smack him on the shoulder like an old friend. He stands, startled and confused. I gesture to my badge. "Ted, from the home office? Ah, I don't expect you remember me. I'm sure all us office dorks look the same. Hey, Sandy sent me down here. Corporate decided to do some big promotion and has really bumped it up online and on the radio. I'm sure you're sick of hearing the commercials already."

Andrew pulls the earbud out of one ear. "How you doing, Ted? No commercials for me. I just listen to this thing."

"Smart." I nod to the iPod. "As for how I'm doing; I'd be fine, except you know what Corporate forgot to do?"

"No." He shrugs.

"Those fuckers forgot to print the contest on the boxes." I hand him a sheet of glossy gold stickers. "I've got to put at least thirty stickers up per store tonight because the damn contest goes live tomorrow.

"Shit. That sucks, man." Andrew looks at the pile beside him. "You want to just grab those three cases on the top? I can shelve another product while you work."

"Sure. Thanks, man." I pound Andrew's shoulder again and pull the boxes he pointed at off to the side. He pulls the second earbud out and we

183

chitchat about office politics that I make up as I go along.

As I put a sticker on the last box, Andrew turns to me. "Hey, are you going to all the stores in Hillsboro tonight?"

"Well, you know Corporate," I comment vaguely.

"I only ask because I've still got the Hank's and Albertson's orders on the truck. If you want to just head out there while I finish up, you can probably shave an hour of drive time out of your night.

"Are you shitting me, Andrew? That would be great."

Andrew smiles. "Anything to help a co-worker. Just make sure that you file an 'Atta-Boy' when you get back to the office tomorrow. I could use another mini-bonus to pick up some new music for the iPod."

"I'll do you one better," I offer. "How much do you drivers usually get when your boss gets a positive comment on you?"

"Twenty bucks."

I pull a prepaid visa out of my pocket. "Well, fuck that. Here's fifty."

Andrew almost yelps with excitement when I hand him the card. "You just made my night."

184

"Hey." I shake his hand before I head to the truck. "The feeling's mutual."

# Ring

The days creep by. No one has called the number on the stickers I placed on the Alphabet Apes boxes and my faith in my scheme is faltering. I tell myself that cereal doesn't sell out overnight after it's been stocked. Parents buy the boxes and take them home to hide in dark cabinets out of reach of the children. I tell myself that it's only a matter of time, that I need to be patient, any other number of reassuring thoughts that do absolutely nothing against the anxiety that builds inside of me.

When the phone does ring, it isn't the phone that I've dubbed the "AA Phone" in honor of the cereal I'm using as bait. It's just my regular cell phone with the now familiar message from the correctional facility down south. I hit the button to accept the charges. The line clicks as it connects, but it is strangely quiet on the other side.

"Dad?"

There's heavy breathing on the other end of the line. He clears his throat and then finally says, "Hen, I've got pneumonia." His voice is weak and raspy.

"Have you seen a doctor?"

"They're talking about taking me to the

hospital," he wheezes. "The staff wants to avoid the security risk of having me in a civilian hospital, but the nurse that's been taking care of me is afraid I won't make it."

"When did it start? You seemed fine at Fantasy." I try to remember how long ago that's been. The snow has long since melted, replaced by the familiar pounding of Portland winter rain. The days have all blurred together. Maybe it's been a week since I've seen him. Maybe it's been two.

"A couple of days after our outing I came down with the flu. It hit me hard even though I got the shot." A coughing fit overwhelms him. The hacking lasts a long time, and when it's finally over his voice is barely a whisper. "I thought I was getting better, but two days ago I woke up and felt like I had a bowling ball tied to my chest. It's gotten worse from there."

"What can I do to help?" I start toward the closet for my coat.

"The best thing you can do is to keep moving forward. I'll have someone let you know when they have me checked in, and then you can come tell me how things are going." His next cough racks him so hard that it resembles crying.

"I'll call Dougy, Dad. He'll get you out of

there." I start to say goodbye but I can tell that he can't hear me so I hang up. I look through my phone until Dougy's number appears and soon the line rings in my ear.

"Peter!" Dougy's voice is almost cheerful. "It's not often I see your number on the caller ID. What's happening?"

"Dad needs to go to the hospital. I don't know if the Sheridan people have told you, but they think he's got a bad case of pneumonia."

"Shit." I hear a rustle through the phone. "Do you think he's faking it?"

I roll my eyes. "The sound of his lungs attempting to exit through his eyeballs is pretty convincing. I need you to make a call and push them to take him in."

"I'm sure they've got it under control, Peter." All of the excitement has drained from Dougy's voice. "They've got some of the best jail medics in the state down there."

"Just call them." A burst of anger pulses through me when he sighs through the phone. "We need him to keep moving forward. He's the only one who knows where the bodies are. If we lose him, we're going to die waiting for people to stumble across all of

188

those other bodies on accident."

Dougy grunts. "I never thought I'd see the day when *you* had to talk *me* into this case."

"Me either. But here we are."

## Timing

Even with Dougy breathing down the FCI Sheridan faculty's necks it takes two more days for them to transfer Dad to a hospital. After 48 hours of anxiously pacing my apartment, I'm relieved to finally be getting in the car to drive down to Salem Hospital.

I pull into a Dutch Brothers Coffee before heading onto the freeway. The barista exudes the kind of enthusiasm that is only achievable after snorting a line of ground espresso. "Radioactive" pulses out of the tiny drive-up coffee booth and I wonder how the neatly groomed skater can even hear me place my order for two large coffees. He does though, and he shouts the order to a tiny woman who could be the next cover model on Portland Monthly Magazine.

"So how is your morning going?" Skater Dude leans out the window at me, smiling as if we chat every day.

"Fine, I guess." The song dies out and is quickly replaced with rhythmic double-bass kicks and melodic screams. I nod toward the shop. "I can never understand what these kinds of singers are saying."

The guy laughs. "Well, it would be hard for you to understand these guys. They're from Japan."

"It's a pretty intense track for nine in the morning."

"No man, they're great. The band is called Merging Moon. I saw them on Anthony Bourdain's 'Parts Unknown'." The guy reaches behind him to retrieve my drinks from the sprightly woman he works with. As he turns toward me she jumps up and down, strumming an air guitar to the gyrating beat of the music.

Skater Dude passes the coffees to me and hands me a stamped frequent customer card. I push a few dollar bills through the window at him. He beams. "Thanks, man. Hope you have an awesome day!"

"You too." I look past his shoulder to the writhing woman behind him. "You guys don't hurt yourselves, now." Their laughter is drowned out by the roar of the speakers. I'm thankful for the silence that envelops me as I pull away and roll up the window.

The road is wet and overflowing with commuters when I pull onto Highway 26. I curse their existence as I follow the signs toward I-5 South and like a true Portlander I busy myself thinking about a time before traffic. Just as I marvel at how the new construction along the side of the highway is changing the landscape of the city once more, a shrill sound fills the car.

It takes a couple of rounds of the high pitched bleating before I realize that it is the sound of a ringing phone. I pull off to the shoulder and flip on my hazard lights before I unbuckle and frantically paw through the pockets of my coat. The AA phone vibrates against my fingers and I am able to pull it out and hit the green button before it pushes the call to voice mail.

"Hello?"

"Is this Alphabet Apes?"

I smack myself in the forehead for being so unprofessional. I've practiced this a hundred times. "Yes, sorry. Alphabet Apes contest line. This is Ted. How can I help you?"

"Hey Ted. My box of cereal says we might have won a prize." Children squeal wildly in the background of the call. The woman hushes the rabble. "Sorry about that."

"Hey, that's okay. I'm so glad that you called. You are our first contest winners." I do my best to sound enthusiastic while I simultaneously hunt around the car for a pen and a scrap of paper to write on. The squeals on the other end of the line are so piercing that I have to pull the phone away from my ear.

The woman's shouts are garbled but firm and

soon she returns to the line with a normal tone. "Really, so sorry. The girls are excited to have won. The sticker on the box doesn't say what the prize is. I'm assuming you'll mail us a beach ball or something?"

I think about the mountains of toys and games piled around my apartment. I hadn't considered that contest entrants' expectations for a prize might be so low. I shake my head. "No, Ma'am. We aren't some cheap outfit that sends out little junk like that. We have hundreds of prizes. I'll just need you to bring your cereal box in so that we can pull the secret code and see what you've won."

"Bring the box in? How am I supposed to do that?"

I hadn't expected the woman's suspicious tone and try to sound more confidant. "Yes. See, this is a regional contest. The phone number that you've dialed is for our Portland Metropolitan contest. We have local offices that house the prizes. You simply bring the box in, we scan it for the secret code, and then you walk away with your prize."

"Oh." I can almost hear the woman give me a dirty look through the phone. "This is one of those shopping club membership deals. I come in to get my prize and you sit me down for a three hour sales pitch,

193

then the prize that I've won ends up being a disposable camera and coupons to the movies. No thanks."

The line goes dead before I can think of a way to overcome the woman's objection. I toss the phone aside, frustrated with my lack of finesse. A glint of light catches my eye in my rear-view mirror and I recognize the twirling red and blue as police lights. "Fucking great."

I roll down the window as the officer approaches. He is cautious of the traffic that hurtles by. "Good morning, Sir. Are you having a problem?"

"No, sir. Well, yes, sir. I pulled over to take a phone call."

The police officer stands up straight. He frowns at me, but does his best to not appear annoyed that he has to deal with me. "No car troubles?"

I grin sheepishly. "No, despite the haggard appearance of my piece of shit car, it runs like a champ. My dad's in the hospital. I'm actually on my way there now. I would have ignored the call but I thought..."

The police officer's face softens and he holds his hand out. "Say no more. I lost my dad two years ago. How bad is it?"

"Pneumonia, so who knows? He's in the ICU right now."

"Do you need an escort?" The cop fingers the button on the radio attached to his coat.

"Thank you so much, but I don't think so."

The officer's hand moves away from his radio and down into a side pocket. He pulls out a business card and gives it to me, held between two fingers in the familiar way that smokers offer a cigarette. "If you decide you need to get there in a hurry, just give me a call. This number calls my cell phone direct so you don't have to bother dispatch."

I take the card and nod. "Thank you, Sir."

"I hope things turn around for your dad. Drive safe."

I wait for the officer to get into his car and pull back out into traffic before I start my engine. While he simply flipped on his light bar and the traffic dispersed, I have to crawl along the shoulder for several minutes with my blinker on before I find a break in the traffic wide and slow enough for me to merge. I gun the engine and lurch back onto the highway.

It takes me nearly two hours with traffic to make it to Salem Hospital. I spend the entire time on the road talking to myself about the woman who called to claim her cereal box prize. It was the first call, and I totally botched it.

"I need to bring the box to you?" My voice cracks with the high pitch.

"Yes Ma'am. This contest is being administered to our local customers. The number you've dialed is for our Portland office, making it easier for us to match you with your prize."

"This seems suspicious." I wag my head as I screech the statement.

"We understand that this is different from any contest held by our competitors. We strive to avoid the long waits, lost paperwork and red tape that comes with traditional contests. By having a representative in your area to distribute prizes directly, your award is immediate."

"Are you trying to sell me something?" My nose vibrates with the nasal tone and I rub the tip of it with my hand to get the tingling to stop.

"No Ma'am. Not only are we not going to sell you anything, but there is minimal paperwork to receive your prize. We will require a valid ID, of course. But we will not put you on a mailing list. These prizes are simply a thank you for your continued support of our company."

I decide that's as convincing as I'm going to get for today. I turn on the radio, listening to 94.7 KNRK for as long as the signal will hold out, and then revert back to silence for the rest of the drive. The bitterness of the sludge at the bottom of the second coffee cup is amplified by its lukewarm temperature, but I finish it anyway.

Once I've pulled into the hospital lot and parked, I find my regular cell phone and call Dougy. I ask him where they are. His voice guides me into the secure wing where my dad is being treated.

I find him in the depths of what looks to be a disused hallway, standing in front of a couple of heavy double doors. "So, I hate to admit it, but I'm glad that you called me the other day. He's doing pretty bad. If we would have waited any longer, he probably wouldn't have made it."

I shake his hand and wait as he presses a buzzer. The doors open slowly and I follow him past an abandoned Nurse's desk toward a room with two officers standing guard. They nod at me as I pass by, but all I can see is Dad hooked up to a series of tubes and hoses. He is sleeping, but it is far from restful. His chest barely lifts as he wheezes into the mask tied to his face. Tubes snake across the bed, monitors blip behind him, liquid drips through an IV, and life barely clings to his shriveled body.

"They have him sedated." Dougy moves to the far side of the room and perches himself on a narrow bench below the room's only window.

"Fuck." I sit on a stool next to the bed and take my father's hand, careful not to disturb the IV that sticks precariously out of his paper-thin skin. His fingers are cold. I look up at Dougy and ask, "Can I have some time with him?"

"Sure thing." Dougy wrestles himself back off of the bench. He pats me on the shoulder when he passes by. "I'll be right outside if you need me."

We've been alone in the quiet room for a few minutes when Aerosmith starts to fill the air. There are "No Cell Phone" signs peppered all over the hospital and I rush to answer it before anyone comes in to yell at me for breaking the rules. "Hello?"

The strange voice that called me from the prison a couple of weeks ago responds. "If he dies, we are here for you. We'll help you no matter what." The line goes dead.

"Your girlfriend?" Dad eyes me through one barely open slit. His voice creeps out from under his oxygen mask, then he's overcome with a fit of coughing that lifts him from the mattress. His body contorts with pain until the coughs subside. The blips

198

on the monitor behind him dance excitedly.

I take his hand again and squeeze. "It was just a prank call."

"You don't get many of those these days." Dad sinks down into the pillows behind him and his pale skin seems to disappear into the sheets. "Caller ID messed that up a long time ago."

"People can block their number now. It just shows up as 'Anonymous'." I shrug.

Dougy pushes the door open with his shoulder. He talks to someone in the hall and isn't paying attention to us yet. Dad's trembling fingers squeeze my hand. I lean in close to him so he doesn't have to raise his voice above a whisper.

"How are things going with the project?"

I can't bring myself to tell him that I've botched the only call that I've gotten. "It's going. I've got the stickers placed. Just waiting for the phone to ring."

Dad nods once, and the corners of his mouth curl into half a smile. He pats my hand tenderly. "Have you considered putting out more stickers? Maybe you don't have enough saturation."

I hadn't considered that. "I'll get more made up tonight. I did a couple hundred stickers and got one call. Maybe I'll run a couple thousand tonight and put them out. See what happens."

"That's good. Very good."

"What's good?" Dougy leans against the end of the bed, careful to avoid contact with Dad's feet.

I look at Dad, and we shrug at one another. "It's a good day to be at the hospital," Dad wheezes.

Dougy snorts. "I suppose it's better than being in the clinker. The food's probably better, anyway."

Dad's head falls to one side and then the other. "Nope. Our pudding comes with cookies and whipped cream."

"Of course it does." Dougy's eyes roll to the ceiling and then fall back on me. "How about you?"

"I don't like pudding, so it doesn't matter to me either way."

Dad's chuckle grows until it's lost in another fit of coughing. Dougy moves toward the other side of the bed and takes Dad's hand into his own. For a moment, Dougy looks down at my father as if he were his own. The creases around his eyes soften, and he rubs Dad's hand with tenderness.

Dougy suddenly remembers I'm here and shoots me a guilty look. He pushes off of the bed and lumbers back to his perch on the windowsill. He clears his throat with dramatic flair. "Ollie, you'd better get rid of that cough if we're going to get back to finding bodies."

Dad forces his cough back down into the recesses of his chest. Once he has it under control he pushes the oxygen away from his mouth and croaks, "I'd like to go see the sea lions."

Dougy and I share an understanding nod.

"Well, I guess I'll check with the doctors to see what kind of timeline we are looking at." I get out of my chair and head toward the door. "Keep a good eye on him, Dougy."

"I won't let him out of my sight."

# The Dump

The bank is empty by the time I remember that I am supposed to pick Valorie up for dinner. I press my forehead against the glass door and gaze into the empty lobby. The carpets reflect the soft glow of the dimmed lights. The endless laminate counters and empty desks have all the cheer of an abandoned TV game show set.

There's movement near the back of the lobby and the sudden flash of color makes me jump with a start. Valorie's dress throws itself in front of her as she walks, announcing her approach with alternating patterns of red and yellow. Her face falls a little when she notices me.

She takes her time passing through the empty lobby. She straightens stacks of deposit slips on the counters and returns rogue pens to their holders before she approaches the door. When she finally turns the lock she only pushes the door open a few inches. "Glad you finally decided to show up."

"Sorry. I had a family emergency."

Val's shoulders drop and she leans her forehead against the door. "Uh huh."

"I should have let you know. But to be honest, I just didn't think about it."

Val loses her composure and smacks her hand against the glass. "We've been together for how long now? And you don't even think to call me when there's an emergency?"

"We aren't together." I shock myself with the admission.

Valorie's face turns red. It isn't the deep rouge of passion that I'm used to. The flush of her skin is blotchy, and her eyes begin to swell. "We aren't?"

"I'm in love with someone else." I immediately realize this is the wrong thing to say. "She doesn't know, of course. It's not like I was cheating or anything."

"I don't believe it." Val hangs her head for a moment and then her teary eyes fix on me. Something in them changes and she stares at me with daggers. "I don't believe you. How dare you use me to fill your bed as if I'm some kind of party favor!"

"It wasn't like that. You were turned on and it's been a long time since I've been with anyone. It was just supposed to be a one time thing."

"I see. So, I was a one night stand that lasted too long?"

"Sort of."

Valorie pulls herself to her full height and I

203

think she might spit at me through the crack in the door.

"I think you'd better find yourself another bank."

# Counsel

I'm alone in Jeanne's office. The receptionist told me that she was ready for me but when I got here the room was empty. I fidget in my chair. Without her body lounging in the leather armchair across from me, the whole room feels artificial. I get up and go to the window. Jeanne has a wide angle view of the parking lot. Grey pavement and white lines as far as the eye can see.

The door clicks open behind me and Jeanne slinks in. Her gorgeous eyes lock onto mine and she smiles at me sheepishly. "Sorry I'm late."

I smile back at her and return to my place in the chair across from hers. I spread my hands wide across the smooth arms of the chair and imagine that I'm stroking her bare calves. My fingers draw little circles in the red leather.

She giggles. "You seem awfully happy today."

I consider this for a moment. "Well, Jeanne. I think I am."

"Tell me about it." Jeanne jots a quick note on the pad beside her. She's probably just writing today's date and my name, but maybe she's drawing a little smiley face and writing the word "happy".

"I broke up with that woman I was seeing."

Jeanne's eyebrows shoot up her forehead. "What brought you to that decision?"

"I realized that I was just wasting my time with her. I never really cared about her. She was just there. Even when I didn't ask her to be."

Jeanne nods. "It is good of you to understand the difference between someone bringing meaning to your life versus someone taking up space. So many times people get lonely and begin to fill their lives with relationships that don't have any substance so that they don't have to feel alone." She looks at me with serious eyes. "That is a great step for you. I'm proud of you."

I inch my knee forward in hopes that she will touch it with reassurance. I ache to feel her fingers grip my kneecap. She leans back into her chair instead and busies herself writing notes. I remind myself that she has to keep her professional distance. I can't help but appreciate her dedication to her craft. I hope that she knows that if anything ever happened between us she could trust me to not turn her in to the authorities. I suppose some risks are just too great to take, even with those we love.

"She was upset when I told her I didn't think about her as a viable romantic partner." I do my best to

206

look sullen even though for some reason Val's tears didn't bring me an ounce of regret.

"I'm sure she was. Ending a relationship is very difficult."

"I mean, the sex was good." My mouth puckers as I realize what I've said. Jeanne doesn't look up. She keeps her 'therapist' face on. "There was just no..."

"Emotional intimacy?"

"Exactly." I nod emphatically even though Jeanne still hasn't looked up from her pad of paper. "I couldn't connect with her."

Jeanne's head bobs up, then down. The motion is stiff and measured. She lays down her pen and her eyes look weary when she looks back up at me. "Do you find you have a problem connecting with people?"

I can tell just what she's thinking and I realize that I have to pacify any fears that she might have about us. "Maybe I don't connect with a lot of people. But when I meet someone who is real, who has depth and breadth of personality and consciousness, then I assure you the bond is strong."

Jeanne looks puzzled. "That is a pretty formal way to describe your emotions."

My shoulders droop. "I guess. That's the way it is."

"Well then, I suppose it's a good thing that we connect so well in our meetings." Jeanne's mouth curls up on one side into a half smile.

"It's the highlight of my day, Jeanne."

# Breakfast

I suspect that Dougy has been staying at the hospital around the clock. He's there in the morning when I stop to share the hospital's gloppy gray oatmeal with Dad, and he's there when the nurses come in to tell me that visitation hours are over at the end of the day. Today isn't any different.

I pop my head into the room to find Dougy asleep in a faded armchair beside the hospital bed. He's snoring so loud that Dad has stuffed cotton balls into his ears. Dad is hunched over a book on the bed, turning the pages so quickly that it's hard to believe that he's actually reading.

I tiptoe to the bed and wave my hand low enough that Dad will see the movement and not be startled by my sudden appearance. He looks up, smiles and pulls a bundle of cotton out of one of his ears. "How does the oatmeal look this morning?"

I wiggle the two cups of oatmeal in my other hand. "Looks like Chicken Fried Steak."

"And I bet it tastes like Eggs Benedict."

I laugh as I settle down onto the foot of his bed. The truth is that this last week of him being in the hospital has been one of the best in my life. Aside from the guards outside his doorway, I don't feel any different than any other person visiting a loved one. For a while we can pretend that when they release him from this place we'll be able to resume a normal life the way the other patients and their families will. I toss him an oatmeal and a spoon before popping the plastic lid off of my own.

"So how is it going with your project?" Dad's mouth is full and the oatmeal squishes between his teeth when he talks. I would tell him that he looks disgusting, but I'm just glad to be sharing meals with him.

I look over my shoulder at Dougy, who lets out a snore that makes the chair he's sitting in vibrate. "Do you really think we should talk about this right now?"

Dad bumps my arm with his elbow. "Sure. He was up until nearly three in the morning, worrying over me because I couldn't stop coughing. He'll be out for at least another hour." Dad notices my suspicious look and winks. "I've known Inspector Douglas long enough to know that he needs eight hours of beauty sleep to function. Trust me. As long as his phone doesn't ring, he won't hear a thing."

I stir my breakfast as my stomach sinks. Finally, I put the remaining oatmeal on the tray beside

Dad's bed. "People are calling, but nobody has committed to coming in."

Dad nods between bites. "Are the calls going any better?"

"I guess so. It's taking them longer to hang up on me."

"Well, that's progress." He smiles at me and nudges me with his elbow. "Keep working on your script and you'll have those appointments lined up before you know it."

As if the cereal boxes can hear Dad thinking about them, the AA phone begins to vibrate in my pocket. "There's a call now."

Dad watches me excitedly as I fish the phone out of my pocket. The intermittent buzz tickles my fingers and I hesitate. Dad smiles and I find enough courage to hit the "Talk" button.

"Alphabet Apes Portland Contest Hotline, this is Ted speaking. How can I help you?"

A young voice titters through the speaker. "Hello? Hi, I'm Jesse. My box of cereal says I won a prize. Did I win a prize?"

"Yes, you sure did! We are conducting a regional contest. All we need is for you to bring your cereal box down to our prize office so that we can scan the box and award you your prize."

"So there's just a place I go and then I get something cool?" The voice cracks a bit.

"Absolutely. Do you mind if I ask how old you are?"

"Thirteen. Gonna be fourteen in three days though." The kid lets out a nervous croak. "Am I old enough to win?"

I clear my throat and wink at Dad. "Well, technically speaking I can't release prizes to anyone under the age of eighteen. Do you have a parent or guardian?"

"Oh. Yeah!" I hear a crackle on the line. "My mom doesn't work. She can totally drive me and sign whatever."

"Great. Do you have a pen and a piece of paper?" I pull a pocket notepad out and flip through the pages until I find the list of addresses for the office rentals I have lined up. The kid tells me he's ready and once we figure out which office is closest to him I relay the address. "I have time slots open at two, four and six today, otherwise we'll have to push to Monday. What works best for you?"

"Today, definitely." The kid asks me to hold, then yells at the top of his lungs for his mother. He relays the available times to her and she settles on the two o'clock spot. "We'll be there at two," he repeats as if I didn't already hear the entire exchange.

"Great. What is your name?"

"Jesse Deere. My bros just call me J."

I stifle a laugh. "OK, J. And what's your mother's name?"

"Tracey."

"Great. J, I have you and Tracey down for two o'clock. Please check in at the front desk when you arrive. The receptionist will get you taken care of. Please make sure your mother has a valid form of government issued identification with her." I pause for a minute to make sure Jesse has time to take it all in. Then I add, "Hey, J. One more thing. Don't be late. We've got a lot of winners to meet with, and I've got to run a tight ship. If you're more than ten minutes late, we won't be able to get you in."

I hang up the phone and Dad glows at my performance. He drops his oatmeal onto the tray beside him and practically leaps into my arms. He holds onto me tight and kisses me on the cheek. "See? It was only a matter of time."

As soon as I peel my elated father off of me I call to book a conference room at the temporary office.

I decide to hold it for a block of three hours. I figure that will give me enough time to get back across town, set up a convincing display and be ready to go when Jesse and his mom show up.

I say goodbye to Dad and leave the hospital in a daze. I can't decide if I'm excited that the plan is moving forward, or if I'm going to give all of the prizes away and then abandon the rest of it. I tell myself that I don't have to make a decision about murdering anyone right now. Jesse is just a kid, and he needs his mom. It doesn't matter if I like them or not, I decide that no matter what happens I am just going to give them something nice so we can all move on with our lives.

The whole drive back to my apartment goes by in a blur. I can't help but admit that the way my father reacted to me booking this appointment made life seem suddenly complete. I've spent twenty years trying to convince myself that I didn't need him, but now that he is within arms reach I can't imagine going back to the blandness of living without him.

I back my car up to my apartment building and pile it full of video game consoles, guitars, board games and collectable toys. The trunk fills quicker than I expect it to, and soon I have to pack prizes into the back seat and front passenger seat as well. I somehow

214

get it all to fit, along with my laptop and a dummy UPC scanner that I ordered online. I tuck my fake Alphabet Apes poster into a gap behind the seat and string the lanyard around my neck. "It's now or never."

I cram myself into the car. The feet of a child sized art easel pokes me in the ribs. I do my best to ignore the stabbing wooden legs as I turn the wheel and start out on my journey south toward the Beaverton office building. Traffic slows as I merge onto Highway 217 and I drum on my steering wheel impatiently. Every once in a while I catch a glimpse of people on the highway eyeballing my overloaded car. I cringe at the thought that they all know that I am up to something.

I try to ignore the feeling that they know I'm an imposter. Despite my efforts, I'm afraid that someone will realize that I'm the kind of guy who drives around town in a beat up Honda sedan packed with toys to use as bait. If they figure that out, they'll think I'm a kidnapper. A pedophile. A murderer.

I worry the entire way, but no one stops me. Not a single person on the highway points their finger accusingly or swerves as they pick up their cell phone to call 9-1-1. Nothing happens except that it starts to drizzle and I have to turn my wipers on the intermediate setting to keep them from making the god awful screeching sound of rubber on a not quite wet windshield.

It's only the second time that I've been to the office building. When I see it, I'm struck by how much it looks like a stock photo on the internet. The hedges are perfectly groomed, the building numbers gleam in giant gold letters between the second and third floor and the entire scene is spotless. Not a single candy wrapper flutters across the sidewalk. It's as pristine as one of those Street of Dreams houses that no one has ever lived in. Constructed just for the sake of being beautiful.

I head into the lobby with my arms loaded with stuff. A young man sits behind the reception desk. He's dressed for hipster business in a tailored suit with a trendy skinny tie. He has a fresh clean shave and a swooping haircut that makes me wonder where his hair actually begins and ends. He flips his head to the side as if he's about to have a seizure but then I realize he's just trying to get the wild hair out of his eyes without touching it with his hands.

"Can I help you?"

"Yes. I'm Ted from Alphabet Apes. I've got a conference room booked from one to four this afternoon."

The nest of hair slides in front of his face when he leans down to look at his appointment book. He tries to get it to move by flicking his head a couple of times before he gives up and pushes the whole mass out of his field of vision with his hand. I fight the urge to suggest he see a barber. A male barber. One who has never been to beauty school. The kind of barber that still smokes indoors and learned to cut hair in the military. Yup, I think a bald guy with a freshly sharpened set of clippers could do some good here.

"I have a conference room for you on the third floor." He jots down the room number on a scrap of paper with the hand that isn't holding his hair up. He glances up at me and nods at the stuff in my arms. "Do you have more to unload?"

"I do."

The hair bounces and twirls atop his head as he spins around in his chair. "Let me show you where the service carts are kept."

It takes six trips with the help of a cart to get the car unloaded. Once the last load of stuff is moved, the room I'm in looks as though the mall threw up in it. There are piles of retail therapy on every available surface. I'm glad that I got one of the bigger meeting spaces and I make a mental note to always ask for room large enough for twelve people when I'm booking these appointments.

I pull my phone out of my pocket to check the time. I've got about a half hour before Jesse and Tracey show up. There is a lot of work to do. I start to sort the items into categories, turning each corner of the conference room into its own little department. I decide on an electronics section, arts and crafts, music, and then everything else. The fourth section becomes a mishmash of crap that I never imagined could exist when I was growing up. Astronaut ice cream, Mr. Potato Heads riding dinosaurs and stuffed Siamese cats that look pissed off right out of the box.

"Kids these days." I shake my head.

The final touch is to hang the banner that I had printed at FedEx. I realize that I've forgotten tape, pushpins, or any other device that might help me hang a strip of vinyl from the stark white walls. I lean across the massive conference table and push a button on the angular intercom that is propped up like a decorative centerpiece. It beeps for a minute and then the voice of the swirly haired receptionist answers.

"Sanchez. Front desk. May I help you?"

"Yeah. Hey, Sanchez, this is Ted in room 309.

You wouldn't happen to have any thumb tacks or tape, would you? I've got to hang up this banner..."

"Please, do not use any devices that will leave permanent marks on the wall. No duct tape, push pins, glue or other semi permanent adhesives."

I clear my throat. "Right. None of those. I've got to hang this banner. Any suggestions?"

"Double sided poster tape can be found in the drawer under the whiteboard."

I jog to the edge of the room where a large whiteboard is encased in fancy cabinetry. I open drawers filled with ball point pens, pads of paper, and finally, a single almost empty roll of double sided tape. "Thanks, Sanchez. I got it."

There's no reply and I realize that Sanchez already hung up.

I'm standing up on a wheeled chair, trying to get the banner to hang straight without killing myself when the intercom lets out a long, low beep. My hands are over my head. I press the banner against the wall and realize that I haven't taken the second tab off of the tape to reveal the adhesive. I look under my armpit, back towards the triangle on the table. "Hello?" The intercom beeps again. I realize I've got to push a button to answer the damn thing and let the banner go. The vinyl scrapes against the wall as it falls, draping itself over the toys.

The chair shifts as I scramble down and I lose my balance. I start to fall ass over teakettle but somehow manage to catch myself on the edge of the whiteboard cabinet before I crash to the floor. The intercom beeps at me again.

I stretch to push the flashing red button. My breath is uneven, my heart pounds against my rib cage, and I'm about ready to lay into Sanchez for trying to kill me. I manage a curt, "What?"

"Mr. Willard, your two o'clock has arrived."

I look back at the banner. "Give me ten minutes, then send them up. Tell them I'm wrapping up with another customer."

The chair goes back to the wall and I climb up on it, careful to stay still so the wheels don't take off on me again. I decide not to worry about the banner being even, pull the tab off the adhesive and smack the vinyl against the wall. It holds, and once I've gingerly climbed down again I look back to see "Alphabet Apes" hanging almost level.

I wheel the chair back to the table and hit the space bar on my laptop, bringing it to life. I have the scanner gun set up beside it. The scanner doesn't work, but it does make a convincing beeping sound when you pass it over a barcode. As long as I can keep them from looking at the laptop screen, they'll never know that the beep announces a reader error.

I pull up a spreadsheet with headers labeled "Name", "Date" and "Location of purchase" across the top. It has the same Alphabet Apes logo in the upper left corner as I have on my badge and business cards. The whole setup looks legitimate, and I feel a boost of confidence. This is going to work.

There is a knock at the door. I spring from my seat to open it, but Jesse is impatient and it swings wide before I get there. The kid is short, wiry, and has eyes the size of saucers. He stands in awe of the stuff piled around the room and I can't help but smile for making his day. A tall, round woman approaches from behind him. She seems pissed off and her mood doesn't lighten when she finds Jesse has blocked her path.

"Get in, or get out." She pushes Jesse to the side and forces her way into the room.

I extend my hand. "You must be Tracey."

"Mmmhmm." Tracey turns her back on me. "Well, are you going to give him the box, or what?"

"Oh, yeah!" Jesse swings a knapsack off of his shoulder and pulls a box of cereal out of it. "I'm Jesse.

221

This is my mom. I told her to bring ID like you said. Here's my box. Do I get to pick a prize? This is so cool."

I laugh at his enthusiasm. "Yeah, it is pretty cool. Here's how it works. I'm going to head over to my laptop and scan your box. It will tell me what you've won. Then we'll do a little paperwork, and the two of you will be on your way." I wink at Tracey.

"So this won't take long?" She shuffles her feet and looks longingly at the chairs surrounding the table.

"Not at all, but feel free to pull up a seat." I nod to Jesse. "Want me to give you a tour of the goods?"

"Fuck yeah!" Jesse jumps up on his tiptoes and does a little dance. His jeans dangle from his hips and swish like a hula skirt as he moves.

"Jesse!" Tracey screeches. "Language."

The kid melts back down to the ground. "Sorry. I mean, Yes, Sir. That would be great."

I lean in to Jesse and whisper, "Well then, fuck being quick. Let's take a nice long look."

His eyes sparkle and his grin spreads so wide that I think he'll crack his ears. We turn to the piles of goodies and talk about all of the stuff. We peruse the miscellaneous crap first, and I'm glad when he finds it all as confusing as I do. We look at the mountain of musical stuff and he practically drools over the bright red electric guitar propped up in the center of the display. He reaches toward it and his fingers hover over the strings. Tracey clears her throat in a warning and he pulls his hand back.

"Pretty cool, huh?"

Jesse nods emphatically and I can't help but reach down to uncover the base of the guitar from the pile. I pick it up gingerly and hand it to him. I can see his heartbeat throbbing in the side of his neck. His fingers tremble when he takes it from me. He holds it close to his body as though it were a newborn baby.

"Odds are, it's not going to happen." Tracey announces this with all of the warmth and comfort of a giant pile of dog shit.

Jesse shrugs and hands the guitar back to me.

"Let's see what else there is." I put the guitar back and we move through the art supplies and on to the electronics. I leave him fiddling with an Xbox controller. "So, Tracey. How about we take a look at that box?"

I pick the Alphabet Apes cereal box up off the table. It's lighter than I expect it to be. I flip the top open to find that it's empty. There isn't even a plastic liner inside.

"We didn't know if you had to keep it." Tracey shrugs.

I tap the space bar on my laptop as I sit down. "I'm going to need to see that ID, Tracey."

Tracey digs around her gigantic purse. It's the color of baby vomit and is big enough to carry half a cart of groceries. She produces a smaller purse from within its depths, and from that pulls out a wallet. She flips the wallet open to a long line of plastic cards and pushes the whole mass across the table at me. Her ID is locked behind a plastic screen, pressed so deep into the leather that I bet she'd need a pair of scissors to cut it out.

"Thank you Mrs. Neilson." I read off of her driver's license.

"Miss Neilson," she corrects. She smiles for the first time since they arrived. She smoothes her hair with acrylic fingernails. "Never married."

"I'm sorry for the assumption, Miss Neilson." I shoot her a quick smile and a wink, then get ready to enter her information in the spreadsheet. "Tracey, where did you purchase this box of cereal?"

"I got it at Winco. The one off of Cedar Hills Boulevard." She looks back into her cavernous purse. "Do you need the receipt?"

"No, thank you. Just need to know the general area of town where the prizes are being redeemed for Corporate." I fill in the blanks of my spreadsheet. Then I take a look at the box. My sticker gleams from the lower left corner. It makes me grin. I look over at Jesse. He holds a beginner painter's set, but is distracted by the electric guitar. I scan his box and the computer beeps.

Jesse jumps and Tracey leans forward. I shoot them both a quick smile. "Well would you look at that."

I get up and walk around Jesse toward the guitar. I can feel the energy pulse off of him as I pass and I struggle to keep a straight face. Tracey groans when I touch the smooth red lacquer. Jesse gulps in air and I think he might cry when I simply move the instrument off to the side. I dig in the stack below the guitar stand. I find what I'm looking for and I hand it to him.

He turns the small white envelope over in his hands a couple of times. "What is it?"

"Gift certificates for music lessons."

Jesse's eyes shoot up at me. His eyebrows knit and he trembles before giving in to his excitement and dancing in place. I look over my shoulder at Tracey.

225

"Music lessons?" Tracey sinks back into her chair with a sigh.

"Yes." I turn so I can look at her straight on. I put my hands down on the table and lean forward. It's fitting that we're in a conference room because now I mean business. "These certificates entitle Jesse to five music lessons in the instrument of his choice at Guitar Center. Prizes are not transferable to other people and the certificates are nonrefundable."

"So, the lessons will be at this place?" Tracey waves Jesse over. She takes the envelope from him, opens it, and reads the certificates.

"Yes. They will be right in their store, so the sound doesn't have to bother you at home."

"It's not me." Her hand goes to her chest defensively. "Honestly, it's the neighbors. We live in an apartment. Let's just say that we are on our last legs with the management."

When she hands the envelope back to Jesse, he raises it to his face and stares. "Oh. My. God. I'm going to get guitar lessons." His lips quiver and he whispers, "Ohmygod. Ohmygod. Ohmygod."

I hand Tracey her wallet and offer her the empty box of cereal. She starts to push it back toward me, but Jesse snaps out of his trance and snatches the box off of the table. We both look at him and he beams. "I'm going to keep it. I've got to remember this forever."

I bid them congratulations. Jesse resumes his excited shuffle and dance. Soon I watch the awkward mother and son head down the hallway toward the elevator. I turn to face the room and eyeball the mass of stuff that I have to re-pack to take back home. It has started to rain which complicates things since I want to keep everything looking new. The whole fiasco is going to be a giant pain in the ass.

I think about the look on Jesse's face when he found out that he was getting the one thing he wanted most. I decide it's worth the effort.

# Lies

"So how did it go?" Dougy presses his body into the person in front of us as if he can push the whole line along by force.

"How did what go?" I have to concentrate to keep both plates of Sloppy Joe balanced on the tray. Dougy keeps bumping into me when the line doesn't move and I don't want to drop them. Sloppy Joes were my favorite meal before I got sent into foster care. After that, I didn't have favorites any more.

"Your interview."

My attention snaps. I look at Dougy in a panic. "What interview?"

"Your dad told me that you had a job interview this afternoon." Dougy leans away from me and gives me a long look. "Shit, calm down. It's not like I'm going to tell your boss."

"Oh, that. It went well." I try to hold my sigh of relief in, but it doesn't quite work. A whistle of air passes through my teeth and I wheeze in concert with the lady in front of us. I trip over my own feet when we step forward and almost lose one of the plates. Sloppy Joe sloshes over the edge of the tray and drips down my fingers.

"What kind of job was the interview for?"

"It's a non profit. They give support to needy kids. All kinds of stuff. They have a real nice setup."

We shuffle in silence toward the register, then stop while the wheezy lady in front of Dougy digs around in her hospital bathrobe for enough change to pay for her salad. Dougy pats me on the shoulder. "I'm sure they'll call you back. Don't worry about it."

I cringe under his touch. "Yeah."

"You've just got to build up a little confidence is all." Dougy gives me a wink, then slides up to the counter once Wheezy leaves. He gives the woman behind the register a big smile and extends his hand to her. "Hello there, I'm Inspector Douglas. This is my friend Peter. We're here to work on a big police case."

The woman gives us a thin smile and grips the tips of Dougy's fingers in a weak handshake. "Nice to meet you, gentlemen. Paying together?"

"Separate," we both announce.

She rings us up and we start the long walk to Dad's room. Dougy beams at me. "See what a little confidence can do? She didn't even charge me for the coffee. On the house because I'm an Inspector. A *confident* Inspector. She was practically swooning. It's a good thing that I'm a faithful man. Women throw

229

themselves at me all the time." Dougy turns, serious. "That's one of the many side effects of confidence, Peter."

"I'll try to work on that." I nudge him with my elbow and put on my best straight face. "Hey, Dougy?"

He looks at me as if I'm about to ask him for a long list of pointers. "Yeah?"

I nod to a sign hung over the soda fountain by the exit. "The coffee is free for everyone."

# Caves

Progress has been slow, but Dad's pneumonia cleared up enough for him to be sent back down to Sheridan. Dougy wasted no time in setting a trip up for us to search the sea lion caves in Florence. Yesterday the Sheridan medical staff listed Dad as stable for travel. Today I pack for a few days at the beach.

A winter storm is set to roll in by the weekend. That gives us three days to search the caves and surrounding areas. I'm not sure that this search will be successful. Thousands of people, millions of gallons of salt water and hundreds of sea lions pass through the caves every week. I've voiced my doubts. Dad says that a man by the name of Fisher was left there and Dougy says we're going.

The Oregon coast is mildly comfortable during the heat of summer. It's dark, foggy and dripping with wet during the winter. I've packed every piece of warm clothing that I own into a duffel bag and know that it probably won't be enough. I wonder if someone from Sheridan will have the foresight to send Dad off with a heavy coat and thick pants. He may be a heartless killer, but even murderers can have a relapse of pneumonia.

I update the voice mail message on the AA

phone to let potential winners know that our office is closed until Monday. Satisfied that the message sounds professional enough that someone might leave their contact information, I shut the phone off and hide it inside a loose air vent in the living room. After I reorganize the closets, pull my bed and the couch away from the walls a few inches and shove prizes into every nook and cranny of my apartment they, too, are out of sight.

If anybody breaks in here while I'm gone the only thing that will look out of the ordinary is the stack of mail that has begun to erupt on my dining room table. I think about browsing through the pile of bills while I wait, but the moment I pick up an envelope there is a knock at the door. Dougy is early and impatient to get moving. I toss the electric bill down onto the stack. The pile shifts and slides further across the far end of the table and a single letter drops over the edge onto the floor.

"Anything important in there?" Dougy wrinkles his eyebrows at me like a concerned father.

"I don't know. Is electricity important?"

"Not if you're OK with eating out and taking cold showers." Dougy sees my duffel bag and picks it up. He's already halfway out the door when he calls back, "Do you have everything?"

I pick my coat up off the hook on the wall and jog after him. "If I don't have it, I won't need it."

## The Seal and the Stone

"How did you even get the body down here without anyone seeing you?" Dougy follows the trail back up the hill toward the elevator with his eyes.

Dad shrugs. "It was pretty easy. Fisher made the hike on his own."

We both look at Dad, surprised. I sputter, "He was alive?"

"Sure. And mostly alert." Dad puts his hands in his pockets and rocks back on his heels. "Alert enough to follow directions, anyway. Technically, I didn't even kill him."

Dougy digs at his eyes with his knuckles. He looks as if his brain is about to burst. "What in the hell does that mean, Ollie?"

Dad gazes out over the thrashing water. The sea lions' barks reverberate off the cave walls and he sways as if he's listening to the radio. He gets a glazed look in his eyes while he lets his memory replay everything that happened. "He followed me down here and I told him that the answer to his problems lay with the sea lions. I told him to go to them. That if he searched the cave the answer would come to him." Dad's jaw wiggles as he considers the memory. His eyes snap back to Dougy when he returns to the present. "There were a lot of sea lions that year."

"So let me get this straight. You meet this guy, Fisher, and you get into a conversation where he tells you his life is shit. You tell him that all of the answers to his problems will be solved if he goes to make friends with a pack of sea lions, and he somehow wriggles through the bars, hops over all of these boulders and just disappears?" Dougy's ears burn red. He sweats despite the cold.

"He didn't just disappear. That doesn't happen, and you know it." Dad pulls his hands from his pockets just long enough to make air quotes with his fingers when he says "just disappear". I don't know how he's done it, but he's managed to get Dougy so worked up that his whole head seems to have swelled from the pressure of his building rage. I take a step back.

"Then what happened?" Dougy's hands ball into fists, then he stretches his fingers out wide. He adds, "Without the riddles and suspense."

Dad rocks back and forth on his heels again. "Well, Inspector, we were at lunch and I slipped a little something into his drink to help him be more compliant. Once he was feeling agreeable, we came down here. They were just installing the new safety bars then. The

235

old bars were out of the viewing area and they only had half of the new ones put in. Sure, the gap was roped off, but we ducked the rope so that he could get a better look. When we got to the wall, I told him to climb over and to make his way to the sea lions."

Dougy and I both stand in silence. I can taste the salt in the air as my mouth gapes open and I can't find the strength to force it shut. Dad shrugs.

"To be honest, I thought the fall would have killed him. The stuff I gave him made him too hazy to realize he was hurt, I guess. So he just kept going. Made it to the edge of the pack before one of the big ones noticed him. Then all hell broke loose. Poor bastard didn't stand a chance. When it was over, he didn't look human any more. Everything was obscured by the rocks." Dad shrugs. "I wasn't about to try and go in after him to move him somewhere safer. Sea lions aren't something to be trifled with."

Dougy's mouth opens and closes like a fish out of water. He makes a gurgling sound and I can tell he has something to say, but the words won't come out. I still have my voice though, so I push the question out. "What could you have given him to make him do all that?"

"Rohypnol ."

"You gave the guy roofies?" Dougy's voice cracks when he finally manages to speak. "You didn't drug many of them. Why this guy?"

"I had them on me. He was at the diner, whining that God had abandoned him. I'd been down here with Hen the day before and knew the grating was down." Dad slumps his shoulders with the concern of a noncommittal teenager. "It was convenient."

"You just happened to have roofies on you?" Something between a hiccup and enraged laugh escapes me. "What were you going to do with them? Did you have a frat party to attend later that afternoon?"

Dad eyes me. His face contorts. It takes a minute but he answers me. "You hadn't been sleeping too well. Nightmares had you crying all night. It wasn't doing you any good, and your mother and I weren't getting any sleep."

I feel as though I've been punched in the gut. "You gave me roofies? How old was I?"

"I don't know. Five, maybe six."

I open my mouth but all that comes out is the sound of rushing air. I start to hyperventilate. The cave tilts to one side and I have to bend over and grab my knees to keep from falling over. Dougy grabs my shoulder and together we process Dad's story. The barking of the seals picks up a fevered pitch as if even the animals know how messed up our situation is. A fog horn bellows out on the ocean and the sound ricochets off of the cave walls. The ocean roars through the opening. All of the sounds overwhelm me. "I need to get out of here."

Dougy helps me up and passes me off to another officer up on the stairs. I let the noise of the cave envelop me, hoping that it will drown out any more discussion about my parent inflicted childhood drug use. The panic attack pounding against my heart and flooding my head forces me to look back over my shoulder before I round the corner that leads to the elevator. I can see Dad talking to Dougy. I'm glad I can't hear what he's saying.

# Trouble

Jeanne sets her jaw and studies me. I haven't had much to say yet, and she isn't asking any questions. I fidget under her stare until I can't handle the pressure any more. "Is something wrong?"

Jeanne's lips purse. She starts to shake her head, but stops mid-sway. "A man from the United States Marshals came to see me yesterday."

My breath catches in my chest. I suppose I shouldn't be surprised that he's found out about us, but I had hoped that seeing her this long without any contact from Dougy meant that he wasn't keeping a close watch on me. My mouth twists as I try to find the right words to say. Has he told her who I am? Did he tell her about Dad? I am not sure how to explain the situation without giving away more than I have to. I settle on sitting in silence with a screwed up face.

"Do you know why a U.S. Marshal would contact me regarding your therapy sessions?"

I shake my head, mute. Best to play dumb in situations like this. Jeanne sinks back into her chair. Her slender hands meet and her fingers extend into steeple formation. She presses the tips of her fingers against her lips as she considers me. She looks angelic,

239

similar to an innocent child in prayer. I wonder which deity a therapist might pray to.

"He showed me a picture of you and asked if I knew what your name was."

I do my best to look neutral. "My name is Peter James Wilson."

"That's what I told him." Jeanne's face droops. Lines seep out of the corners of her eyes and trace the edges of her mouth. She looks tired. "He asked to look through your file to see if I had listed any other names for you."

I don't respond. The only sound in the room is the ticking of the clock on the wall. I make a mental note to speed up my plan to buy a digital clock for her. The ticking of the old-fashioned mechanics echo in my brain. I look up at the clock and will the battery to die. The second hand waves at me in defiance as it passes the numbers painted on its face.

"Peter," Jeanne says in a softer voice than I'm used to hearing. "Do you have any history of multiple personality disorder?"

The question catches me so off guard that I let out a burst of laughter. I don't even know how to answer her. Most of the personalities I've ever had were assigned to me by someone sitting behind a desk. The

240

others were schemed up just for fun. "No," I answer. "I'm fairly certain that I've only got the one."

Jeanne leans forward. "Have you ever experienced hallucinations? Found yourself surrounded by people or things that you discovered later did not really exist?"

I can feel my eyebrows press against one another as I try to figure out where her questions are heading. "I don't do drugs."

"That's not what I mean, Peter. I'm talking about when you haven't been drinking and haven't been prescribed any medication."

My hands unfold and I lay them out in my lap, palms up. "I don't think I've ever had a hallucination aside from when I was nineteen and had my wisdom teeth pulled. They had me so doped up that I thought I had hamsters in my mouth. They turned out to be cotton balls."

Jeanne's mouth cracks the tip of a smile, then she bites her lip to keep things serious. "I really want to believe you, Peter, but the man who came to see me made me wonder if you have had a history of instability."

"He said that?" My eyebrows shoot so far up my forehead that I have to rub them with my right hand

241

to get them to settle back into place again.

"Not in so many words. But he did ask me several times if you had ever mentioned having a previous life. He asked me about places you may think that you've lived, or other names you think you have had." Jeanne finally starts to relax. Her hands fold neatly in her lap and she tilts her head. "Do you know him?"

"That depends. Was he awkwardly confident, flirty and a little bit arrogant?"

Jeanne nods.

"Sounds like Inspector Douglas to me."

She lets out a sigh and the sound washes over me with the serenity of falling rain. I forget what we're talking about and I imagine her lying beneath me, sighing with pleasure as I trace her shoulders with my lips.

"So you've dealt with him before?"

I snap out of my fantasy. "Yes. For most of my life, actually."

Jeanne leans forward. She presses her elbows into her knees so hard that it makes an indent in her slacks. "Peter, are you in trouble?"

I chuckle a bit. I can't help it. It's obvious that Dougy hasn't told her anything. Maybe he's just

242

covering his ass. At this point, why he's bothering Jeanne doesn't matter. He's breached my defenses again and now I've got to figure out if it's worth fighting back or not.

"Jeanne, if I wasn't in some kind of trouble, I probably wouldn't need therapy."

# Confrontation

The gray walls of the visitation room have stopped making me uncomfortable. Knowing that I've been at the prison often enough to feel normal about it does, though. I have found that sitting in the metal chair sideways, leaning against it with my elbow propped up on the back is the most comfortable way to sit. I sprawl out like a preppy white boy doing a terrible impersonation of a gangsta. I feel ridiculous, but at least my back doesn't hurt.

No matter how often I come to see Dad here, I never forget that every word we speak is monitored. Today, Dougy visits another inmate three tables over. There's no way that nosy bastard would miss a chance to listen in on our conversation.

"He crashed my therapy sessions again." I don't even have to mention his name. Dad knows who I mean and he looks down the short row of chairs at Dougy to acknowledge the breach.

"Privacy is an illusion. It took me a long time to realize that."

"I'm sure the rectal inspections are a good reminder." I laugh at my own joke and Dad grins.

"You aren't wrong. So what was it he found

out?"

I gesture with my thumb towards Dougy's back. "I'm pretty sure he found out that I still haven't told anyone that I am your son. Or that I even know you. Or that there is any universe in which our paths might have crossed."

"Well, keeping it to yourself is all you can do until it's over." Dad's shoulders shrug as if he's telling me I still have to go to gym class even though I don't want to change clothes in front of other people.

"Maybe I'm tired of keeping it to myself." I jump when my fist slams down against the steel table top. I don't even remember lifting my hand , but I can feel the vibration of the impact all the way up my shoulder. It feels as though my anger is pushing steady and hard at the backs of my eyes, making them bulge out at my father.

An officer steps away from the wall. "Sir, you can't do that in here."

"Do what? Be pissed off that I'm busting my ass to help all of you, and the only reward I get is to have my integrity questioned?" My cheeks puff and I can feel the veins in my neck pulse.

"Calm down, Sir." A second officer creeps closer with a hand on his hip. He grips his belt where

245

the pepper spray sits.

"Are you seriously going to spray me down?" I stand up so quickly that the chair skids a few inches before falling over.

"They've been known to use 'reasonable force' for less, Son." Dad's voice is steady, but the warning in his tone is clear.

"You can't bully me. I don't belong here." I look down at Dad. His calmness makes my blood boil. He may be used to letting other people lead him through life, but I've earned my freedom. I've kept my head down all these years just as they asked me to. "I'm a good guy. A decent human being. I don't deserve to be treated like a criminal. Not by this guy, and not by the a-hole pretending he isn't listening to every goddamn word I say."

The second officer stops mid stride. He holds one hand out toward me as if he's a traffic cop stopping cars while his other hand moves away from his pepper spray and toward his cuffs. Dad looks up at me and raises a single eyebrow. "Are you sure about that?"

That's when I lose it. All of the years bouncing around from foster home to foster home. The last five therapists closing their files and locking their doors on me when the pressure of law enforcement got too intense. Having to hide every facet of my past from the people I knew twenty years ago, that I know now, and that I'll undoubtedly meet tomorrow. I've given up every part of who I am, and now I want to take it all back.

"Yes, Dad. I am fucking sure. I haven't done anything wrong, but all of you are intent on treating me like some kind of blabbermouth who can't keep a secret." I turn to Dougy. His back is to me, but his head is tilted so I know he's listening. "Well, Fuck You. You stuck up, ignorant, limp dicked fuck."

I'm so amped up that I don't feel the officer at first. Before I know it, he's got my hands pulled behind my back. He yanks me towards the door, and each time he heaves against me, my shoulders feel as if they will burst from their sockets. I yell for him to stop, promising to leave on my own. He doesn't listen.

None of them have listened to me for so long that I scream. I let loose every wail that I held in as a kid. I release every frustration that I've kept stowed away while being led through a system that focuses on getting more from its perpetrators than it is willing to give to its victims. I curse Dougy, my dad, and every other person that's ever been involved with covering up who I am and who I want to be. My legs thrash out from under me and I fall against the officer. We writhe on the floor together until the second officer joins us.

Officers three and four aren't far behind. Soon I am sprawled as flat as a pancake. There are no less than six hundred pounds of pissed off Corrections pressing me into the floor and I can't get enough air in my lungs to shout that I give up. I don't have enough breath to tell them that they have won, and I will yield because it is the only thing I know to do. They have me in their grasp, and I know deep within me that they may never let me go.

With the little clarity I have left, I wonder if I'm being smothered or if my foggy vision is just my own reflection in the polished boots that stand a half inch from my face. I let myself relax, becoming dead weight that sinks into the concrete. Hands grab my shoulders and hoist me up to get me out of the room. I hear Dad's chair scrape across the floor and when I try to open my eyes I see a blurry orange jumpsuit standing where I think the table might be.

"Well Inspector Douglas," Dad notes, "I think you've made the boy upset."

# Getting Out

I open up one of the closets in my apartment and stare at the mass of toys stacked to the ceiling. There is so much stuff. I know there is more in the closet in my bedroom. Under my bed. Behind the couch. Stuffed behind my entertainment center.

"What the hell am I doing?"

I don't know how I let my father, a confirmed crazed maniac, talk me into all of this. I'm not him. I don't want to be like him. This has to stop before it goes any further. I'm not in the business of luring people to their death. I'm not a cold blooded killer. I may not know who I am, but I sure as hell am not the fiend that he wants me to be.

I pull the toys out of the closet and pack them into grocery bags. When the closet is empty and I'm out of small plastic bags, I find a box of forty gallon trash bags and start to fill them with the other prizes. I'm going to pull the plug on this whole operation.

I'm working on the stash of video game consoles under my bed when the AA phone rings. I try to ignore it but just as it cuts off to go to voice mail it starts to ring again. The sound hits me in the ears with the pounding of a jackhammer, so I dig it out of my pocket and answer.

"Hello?" My greeting is curt. I am not feeling friendly.

A girl's screech hits me in the side of the face. "Oh my God! They answered! Hello? Alphabet Apes? I got a box that says I'm a winner!"

"That is great but-"

"What do I need to do to collect my prize? I saved the box. Do you need me to mail part of it to you?" Her teenage voice teeters on the edge of another scream. "I've never won anything before."

I look over in the corner at the red electric guitar that Jesse held so tenderly. I am ready to let go of all of this stuff anyway, and I guess it wouldn't hurt to let this girl have her pick of the lot. Maybe if I can make her happy, the way I made Jesse happy, I'll feel good again. Damn, at this point in my life I would do just about anything to feel good again.

"The contest deadline ends this week." I slump away from the garbage bag of toys I'd been filling. "You called just in the nick of time."

The girl whoops into the phone which forces me to smile. "So what do I do next?"

"This is a regional contest by Alphabet Apes, so we have offices throughout Portland where you can redeem your prize. You just need to bring us the box, so we can scan it to see what you've won. A valid government issued ID, or a parent and their ID if you are under eighteen."

"I turn eighteen on Friday."

"Happy early birthday." I dig the small notebook and pen out of my pants pocket and flip through the pages. "Let me see which of our offices are closest to you. We can set up the appointment for Friday if you want, so you can get your prize on your birthday."

She screeches again, delighted that her first act as an adult is to win a prize. We discuss the area of town that she lives in and I give her the address of the office near there. I'm just about to end the call with her when the line beeps. I pull the phone away from my face and the screen blinks at me. *Answer Call Two?*

"Lindsey, I'm sorry to cut this short but I have someone trying to grab my attention. I'll see you Friday afternoon. Don't forget to bring your driver's license." I don't wait for her to respond, just hit the button to answer the second call. "Hello, this is Ted from Alphabet Apes. Can I help you?"

Another teenager, male, is on the line. He sounds almost as excited as Lindsey. Just as I'm jotting down his name in the pad, the phone beeps again. Another call.

The phone rings practically off the hook the rest of the night. Moms, dads, kids and teenagers fill my notebook. Before I know it, I have appointments booked through the end of the week and into the next at three different offices. I leave the prizes stuffed in the plastic bags and try to pack up the rest of them between calls. I feel lighter. Things are turning around. I'm going to be a prize wielding hero.

I don't have to be a bad guy at the end. I can just keep meeting people until all of the stuff is gone. Then I can go back to work. Maybe I'll break things off with Jeanne and call Val back. Then everything can go back to the way it was before I got involved with Dad. I can try to be normal again.

My cell phone, the one that is contracted in my name for the next eighteen months, starts to play its familiar tune. It hasn't rang since I left the prison. I imagine it's Dougy calling to plead with me to come back. Maybe it's Dad calling to apologize. But when I pick it up, the phone number doesn't blink across the screen. There is no name attached. It just keeps ringing.

"Hello?"

"We heard about the way things went down.

252

We are still here to help you. If you need us, we will be watching. We will know." The creepy voice mumbles these words at me as if the caller is afraid someone might walk into the room and hear him.

"I don't know who you are, but you need to leave me alone." The voice doesn't reply. "I'm serious. I don't need your help. I'm not involved with Ollie anymore, so if you're trying to get a story out of me you can just stop."

There is a heavy sigh on the line and the voice whispers, "We will be here, if you change your mind. Goodbye, Henry Roberts."

The call disconnects. I consider calling the police. Maybe they can trace my account to find out who is calling. Then I remember the first call, the one from inside the penitentiary. I scroll through my contacts and hit the call button.

"Hello? Peter?"

"Dougy, just shut up. I'm not coming back. I don't want to hear an apology or an explanation or whatever it is you're about to say. Just listen. I've got someone prank calling me. It's happened a few times and now they say they're watching me. Some of the calls are coming from inside Sheridan."

"You're sure?"

"Positive. The first call came in collect."

"Get me a copy of your phone records for the last 90 days. If you can remember which calls are the prank ones, let me know their time stamps. I'll find out what's going on."

I nod into the phone. "Thanks, Dougy."

"Anything for you, Peter."

# Circus

I've done such a good job at telling the prize recipients to not be late that everyone is early. The office's waiting area is so packed with kids that they overflow onto the sidewalk outside. I knew I had booked a lot of appointments on paper, but seeing the bodies crammed into the four seat lobby is completely different from looking at their names listed on paper.

"Excuse me," I say as I weave through the bodies. I do my best not to drop anything. "Prize guy coming through." The people clap and cheer. I feel like Santa Claus.

I have to make several trips and before long a couple of young people volunteer to help me. They do their best not to snoop into the bags but I can tell the temptation is overwhelming. When we've moved the last load into the conference room I reach into my jacket pocket and pull out two twenty-five dollar Visa gift cards.

"Here." I hand the kids the cards. "Now tell everyone to give me a half hour to set up, and we can get this show on the road."

The teens let out a whoop, give each other high fives, and race down the hallway to deliver the message.

I start stacking prizes and amaze myself at how much quicker the sorting goes this time around. Twenty minutes later I've got the prizes laid out, the banner is hung, and I'm booting up my laptop.

I hit the button on the intercom system and tell the receptionist that I'm ready for my first appointment. Then, I wait.

# Center Stage

The AA phone hasn't stopped ringing for three days. It has gotten so bad that I've had to turn it off just so that I can get through the appointments I already have set. I dedicate two hours of the day to doing call-backs. The response is overwhelming.

The exhaustion at the end of the day feels good. I'm excited to wake up in the morning. I can't wait to see the kid's smiling faces. Their parents' relief at their offspring's happiness. The teenagers' delight in not being told "no". It is exhilarating in a way I can't describe, and is dampened only in the knowledge that the piles of toys are getting smaller.

There's only one thing to do. I have to get more prizes.

Maybe this could be my 'thing'. There is a guy that they talk about on the news who wanders the streets of Portland dressed like a homeless person, handing out $100 bills to anyone who offers him lunch or a warm drink. There is a family who adds another table's meals to their tab whenever they go out to eat. Maybe I could be one of those people. I could just be known as "The Prize Guy". Anonymous do-gooder extraordinaire.

I know eventually the money will run out. I'll have to go back to work, but I had planned on going back to work anyway. Maybe I can do this prize thing every time I get a bonus. Or whenever I get a pay raise. A hobby to do in celebration of my own good fortune. My cheeks ache with the effort of so much smiling, but it's a pain that I don't want to end.

I haul the prizes out to my car, ready for another day of babbling children. I almost lose the three boxes I have stacked in my arms when I reach the parking lot and find Dougy leaning against the corner of the building. I recover my hold on the boxes and duck my head down to avoid his gaze. He saunters toward me slowly while I rearrange my trunk to get the boxes to fit.

He touches my shoulder from behind. I refuse to turn around to face him. "What do you want?"

"I know what you're doing." His voice is cold.

I look over my shoulder just enough to see the edge of his face. "And what's that?"

"You haven't answered your phone in a week. You're avoiding me. Avoiding Ollie." Dougy takes a step back and kicks the curb. "You're just going to give up? One bad trip to the beach and it's over for you?"

I unbury myself from trunk and face him. I

258

stand up as tall as I can, but Dougy's bald head still gleams down at me. "One trip to the beach? Maybe it's the father who drugged me to make me shut up. Maybe it's the Inspector who crashes my therapy sessions. Or a lifetime of pretending to be something I'm not just so that I can keep someone else's goddamn secrets."

I slam the trunk lid shut and stomp toward my apartment to make sure I haven't forgotten anything.

"I found out who has been calling you," Dougy's voice cracks.

I spin around. The tension in my legs causes my knees to lock and I almost tip over.

Dougy clears his throat. He looks around as if he's trying to make sure that no one else is listening. A young family spills out of an apartment a few doors down. The parents bicker and their children squeal at one another. Dougy jumps the curb and trots closer to me.

"There is a group dedicated to serving your father," he whispers when he reaches me.

"What do you mean?"

Dougy's face squirms as the words fight to leave his mouth. "Your dad has a bit of a fan club."

I stare at Dougy. He may as well just told me that the Yankees were heading to the Super Bowl. "The

259

fuck he does."

"Lets go inside and I can tell you about it over some coffee. I don't want to talk about it where someone might hear us."

I shake my head twice. "I have an appointment."

Dougy turns to eyeball the boxes in the back of my car. "You aren't moving, are you?"

"I'm not allowed to move without notifying my case worker." I decide not to double check the apartment and pull my keys out to lock the door instead. "I really have to go."

Dougy grabs my arm and pulls me toward him. His face pales. I can't tell if he's going to drag me away or throw up on me. "This club worships your dad and they had someone inside. One of the club's lead members was a corrections officer. He was trying to arrange a way for inmates to join from prison."

My face aches from the scowl I give him. "Did you get him?"

Dougy nods.

"Then I've got to go. Someone is waiting for me."

260

# Cheat

My last appointment of the day is with a man named Glen. The excited conversations that I've had on the phone the last couple of weeks all blend together, but I remember the phone call with Glen. He was pushy. He demanded that I mail him his gift instead of making him travel across town to pick it up. He hung up on me when I told him that mail wasn't an option, then called back again to book the appointment.

I've been excited to see the face of every other winner, but Glen makes my stomach swirl. I jump when the intercom buzzer sounds and have to force my hand to hit the button to answer it.

"Mr. Willard, your four-thirty is here."

"Send him up." I get up to arrange the prizes on the table while I wait. Something about this guy makes me nervous. I check to make sure my badge is level and straighten the stack of business cards beside my laptop. The door swings open and my breath catches in my chest.

The man who enters is not the man I envisioned Glen to be. I thought that he would be big, encumbered in a fitted suit with a high dollar stick planted firmly up his ass. The guy who enters is

261

definitely big, but not in the gym-addicted way I expected. His belly spills over his sweatpants. His plaid shirt is only buttoned halfway and the tails wave in front of him like peasants announcing their coming king.

The man scratches at his wiry beard as he stands just inside the door and takes in the display. He looks over his glasses at me and grunts a hello, then eases himself into the room. He only causes a minor avalanche when he passes the side table loaded down with art supplies. He doesn't notice the tumbling paint brushes in his wake, just fights his way into the chair at the end of the table.

"You must be Glen." I get up from my chair and extend a hand in greeting. He waves noncommittally at the gesture.

"Yeah, that's me. I don't shake hands. Measles."

"You have Measles?" My hand recoils unconsciously and wipes itself on the front of my jacket.

"No. And I don't intend to catch them."

I nod at Glen only because I don't know what else to do. We sit in silence until I remember my script. "Welcome to the Alphabet Apes Portland prize center.

Thank you for coming down here. I know it was a bit of an inconvenience."

"I had to borrow a car. I would have taken the bus but you didn't tell me how big the prize was going to be." Glen eyeballs the red electric guitar that is still the centerpiece of the music section. I promise myself that Glen will not walk away with it.

"Well I am glad that you were able to work that out. Now, I'm going to need to see your prize box so that I can scan it and we can figure out what you've won." I busy myself with waking up my laptop while I wait for him to produce the box, but Glen doesn't move. He doesn't even speak. Just sits there scratching something under the table. I hope it's his knee, but I'm pretty sure it's not. "Glen?"

"Yeah." His gaze shifts from a pile of neatly arranged gift cards.

"Did you bring the cereal box with you?"

Glen shrugs and grunts. He leans back deep in his chair. "I forgot it."

"You forgot it?" The butterflies in my stomach die. They boil in the building lake of acid in my stomach. "It's one of two things that you need to claim your prize."

"I brought a receipt. That's good enough." Glen

263

pulls a wrinkled and stained strip of paper from somewhere below his waistline. He wads it up into a ball and throws it at my laptop.

"Except that it's not." I poke at the loose corner of the receipt ball until it rolls away from me far enough that I can't smell the sweat soaked into the paper.

"Are you serious? It's a proof of purchase."

"We appreciate that you have purchased our cereal, Glen. But only certain boxes were marked as winners. The only way for me to discover what you've won is to scan the box."

"Obviously I had a winning box. I called you."

I consider his logic, but decide to stick with my script. Everyone else has brought their box without question. This guy can't force the rules to fit his scruffy existence. "I understand that you called, but the prize code is on the box. I can't match you with a prize without it."

Glen snorts. Drool escapes his mouth and gets caught in his beard. "I knew this was a scam."

"It's not a scam, Glen. You bring in the box. I scan the box. I take a quick look at your ID and you walk away with your prize. I explained all of this to you on the phone."

He heaves himself out of his chair and waddles around the far side of the table. He fingers a couple of video game cases. "You didn't explain anything. Just said to come down to get my prize."

I know that I told him what he'd need to bring with him. I tell everyone the same thing. "I can't just let you take a prize. I'm sure your kids will be disappointed, but if you want to schedule an appointment to come back with the box I'm sure we can get this sorted out. I have a spot open on Tuesday afternoon if that works for you."

An even louder snort roars out of Glen's thick sinuses. "What kids?"

"Aren't you here to pick up the cereal prize for your kids?" Glen shakes his head. I offer him another out. "Niece or nephew?"

"Look. There's no kids in my family. This prize is for me. I bought the cereal." He moves over to the fiery red guitar and fingers the strings clumsily. It shifts on its stand and he grabs the neck to straighten it. "This kind of stuff is wasted on kids anyway."

"It's better than the cheap stuff that our competitors give out." I try to smile. "So will Tuesday work for you?"

"None of this shit is branded." He moves on to

a stack of tablets and shuffles through their boxes.

"Excuse me?" I can feel the blank expression taking over my face.

"Branding. People on eBay want branded items. Alphabet Apes cups and shirts and stuff. Where's the logo?"

"I'm sorry. Did you say people on eBay?"

Glen shrugs. "A guy's gotta take advantage of every opportunity. Branded merchandise pulls top dollar, especially when it's rare. This being a regional contest? Whew! That's as rare as it gets. People on the east coast are going to go apeshit over this stuff." He chuckles at his use of 'apeshit' while standing in an Alphabet Apes office.

When I don't respond, he becomes more serious. "I'm saving up for an on screen used Daryl Dixon crossbow." Glen practically glows when he looks at me. "It's going to round out the archery portion of my cinematic weaponry collection."

I do my best to smile. "Sounds pretty cool. Maybe you could tell me more about it when you come back next week."

"Tuesday." Glen's grin fades. He looks down at the tablets again. "Think you'll have any branded merch next week?"

266

"I'll see what I can pull together for you."

# Heart Attack

I doubt that Glen is going to show up on Tuesday with a cereal box. If he somehow manages to get his hands on one between now and then, I'll be damned if he's going to walk away with one of the prizes. I stand in my living room and stare at the dwindling heap. All of these toys and games are insignificant to him but they mean the world to the kids and families. I won't let him rob those people of their moment of happiness.

I consider just not showing up for his appointment. I could call the other six people I have booked for Tuesday and tell them that we've switched offices for the day. It would take some effort. I imagine Glen arriving at an empty office. I can almost see the red discoloration of his skin, starting under his beard and creeping up his puffy cheeks. He would be furious. The thought makes me smile.

It wouldn't work out though. Glen is the type of guy who will get so mad that he'll get online and look up the Alphabet Apes corporate office. He'll call them and demand his prize. They won't know what he's talking about but he'll push the issue and there will be an investigation. Maybe they'll run a news story about it, but not the kind where they might call me a philanthropic hero. A family will step forward and tell them how they won. They'll find the fake prize boxes on the shelves of some store. Probably a New Seasons Market. People who shop there are overly concerned about the ingredients in their food so not many of the sugary cereal boxes have been purchased yet. The company will pull the boxes and then there won't be any more phone calls. No more winners. No more smiles.

Glen won't just take the prizes away from the kids. He'll take this happiness from me. This prize giveaway is the only thing I've ever been good at. It's all I have that brings me joy on a continuing basis. Although the contest is fake, the pleasure on both sides of the table is real. The entire scheme has shifted into something that I had never expected it to be. It's a joyous gathering of families in which I get to make one of their small wishes come true. The effort of hauling this stuff around town, setting appointments with strangers and crawling out in the middle of the night to mark more cereal boxes is being repaid with the possibility that I am changing someone's life for the better. Giving them opportunities that, as a kid, I only ever wished for on sleepless nights under the roofs of strangers.

I think about Jesse, who by now has surely had a couple of guitar lessons. I'm sure he loves them and soon he'll be able to play along with the songs he hears on the radio. He's old enough to get the itch to start a band with some friends. Maybe they'll be really good together and get a few gigs. It isn't unheard of for Portland bands to get enough of a following to go on tour. Maybe he'll get picked up by a big production company and make a dent in the music world.

I can't let Glen take away Jesse's opportunity to play guitar. I can't let him ruin my chance to connect with kids who will one day become painters or video game designers. Their entire future may hinge on their meeting with me. They need the magic of our encounter to remain intact. I need to know that I can make a difference. I have to find a way to satisfy Glen so that he'll crawl back into whatever hole he came from.

My breath comes in abrupt bursts one right after the other. My vision blurs and I can feel the floor tilt beneath me. I realize that I'm hyperventilating. I reach forward to find something to support myself with but there is nothing. My arms swing wildly and I stumble forward until I find the edge of the couch. I heave myself over the furniture's arm and land on the cushions in a crumple. My ears ring and my chest contracts. My thoughts muddle until all I can think about is the fact that I might be dying. Glen is going to ruin my entire plan by killing me and he doesn't even know it.

I clutch my chest and look at the clock on the wall. Twelve seventeen in the afternoon. I don't think my rasping breaths can come any shorter but when I think about how shallow and quick they are the panic grips me further and then it seems they disappear. Darkness creeps along the edge of my vision and I can feel myself dying. I force my lungs to inhale one gulping breath and then it all goes dark.

## Cleanup

I don't know when the panic attack ended but when I finally regain consciousness it is dark in my apartment. Pale yellow streams of light pour through the cracks between the blinds in the window and paint stripes on the carpet around me. My head pounds, my body aches, but at least that means I'm still alive.

I roll over and my clothes cling to me. I feel as if I've run a marathon and although my clothes are dry they hold the clammy stench of having been recently drenched with sweat. It takes a couple of tries to get my feet under me, but I finally get up and make my way to the bathroom. I need a shower and some medicine to relax my muscles and clear my head.

I start the water in the shower and pop a couple of pills while I wait for the temperature to even out. I undress and stand naked in front of the mirror. I've felt vibrant and alive for the last couple of weeks but now my reflection is blotchy. I look older than I did this morning.

The hot water stings. I adjust the heat until it's bearable and stand under the water until the ringing of my ears is overwhelmed by the hiss of the shower, and the burning of my lungs is soothed by the steam. I stare absently at the rack that hangs from the neck of the shower head. Living alone, there isn't much in here aside from my body wash, shampoo and a disposable razor. My tired brain reads the back of the bottles for no reason other than that they sit at eye level.

The instructions are the same on practically every bottle of body care product that I've ever seen. I wonder why they even print them. Get wet, apply product, scrub and rinse. Repeat if you have to, move on with your day if you don't. My eyes move down to the long list of ingredients. Methylisothiazolinone. Methylchloroisothiazolinone. Cocmidopropyl Betaine. Oxidized Polyethylene. Sodium Laureth Sulfate. Sodium Benzoate. Sodium Hydroxide. Ferric Ammonium Ferrocyanide.

My brain halts. I grab the bottle of body wash and trace my finger over the ingredients. I feel the adrenalin pulse under my skin and my eyes focus. Ferric Ammonium Ferrocyanide. I shut off the water and leave the bathroom with the plastic bottle in hand. I drip water all over the apartment but I don't have time to think about that right now. I find my laptop and prop it open. I type my question into Google: *Is Ferric Ammonium Ferrocyanide the same as cyanide?*

I click on the second link on the page and read.

*Ferric Ammonium Ferrocyanide is a chemical commonly used as a colorant in bath and beauty products. It produces a blue or yellow color depending on the presence of other reactive compounds. It is related to Ferric Ferrocyanide, commonly referred to in cosmetics as "Prussian Blue", but is not the same chemical. It belongs to a class of inorganic cyanides. If inhaled or ingested, immediately transport the victim to a hospital for medical treatment.*

There is fucking cyanide in my soap. I chuckle at the bottle. No wonder they don't want you to drink the stuff. I lean back on the couch and the chuckle grows into a laugh. I can't believe it. Cyanide in my goddamn apartment. The laughter overwhelms me and I double over. Tears well in my eyes and soon they stream down my face. They probably drop off my cheeks onto my naked knees but I'm still so wet from the shower that I don't feel them fall. A whoop of excitement escapes my chest.

Glen may think that he's going to fuck up my world, but I know just what to do to make sure he doesn't.

# Science

I stare at my laptop. I can't believe that I Googled cyanide compounds from my apartment. I've been so careful up to this point and a slip up like that could mean big trouble for me. I do my best to delete the history even though I know that Google has probably already tagged my IP address for suspicious activity. If anyone ever asks me about it, I decide can just tell them I was worried about poisoning myself. It isn't a total stretch. I live in Portland and everyone here is worried about what chemicals might leech into their bodies. There's nothing more for me to do about my impulsive web browsing so I decide not to worry about it. I make a note to buy some all natural, fragrance free, organic body wash the next time I'm at the store to make the story stick.

If I am going to try to poison Glen, I've got to do some research. I could always go back to Goodwill and see if there's another laptop to pick up but shopping there is hit and miss. I decide instead to go to the library to use one of their public computers.

I rifle through my dresser until I find a stack of library cards. One of the benefits of a lifetime in Witness Protection is the plethora of identities you have to choose from. Most of the cards are for identities that were assigned for me, but some of them are for names of people I made up. I've never been much of a criminal but, since I was a teenager, falsifying documents to check out library books has been a bit of a hobby. Keeps me from having to pay late fees, anyway.

I find a card that has been dormant for a couple of years. The name Neil Apollo is printed neatly on the front, and a signature scrawled with my off-hand is scratched onto the raised label on the back. A faded yellow sticky note tacked to the card reminds me that Neil is an adventurer, an avid researcher of oddities, and volunteers at understaffed schools. Neil's specialty is performing science experiments that seem like they could be magic tricks. I nod at the card and tuck it into my back pocket.

Before I leave the apartment I make myself some breakfast. I smile at the tinkling sound of cereal hitting the bottom of the glass bowl when I pour myself a serving of Alphabet Apes. After I eat, I pack myself a lunch just in case my day of studying gets away from me. I'm gathering up my wallet and keys when my cell phone rings. Dougy's number scrolls across my screen. I'm not over being used by Dougy and Dad, but do feel jovial this morning so I answer.

"Hey Peter." Dougy's voice is hushed. "I'm down at the prison. Ollie says he's willing to let go of three more bodies if you'll come."

"Not interested," I quip as I lock my apartment door.

"Look, I know you're pissed. But you're the one who talked me into getting back into this thing the last time I wanted to walk away. I know this is important to you because, well shit. It's important to me and we are a lot alike, you and I."

"Dad will tell you where the bodies are eventually if he really wants to give them up."

Dougy sighs into the phone. There's a scratch on the receiver when he moves around then his voice comes back clear. "He won't. He's irritated that we're prosecuting that corrections guy who prank called you. Apparently Officer Cult-Follower was smuggling in comfort items for your dad and life has gotten less cozy without him."

The Portland skies spit a drizzle of rain at me when I cross the parking lot to my car, and I have to tilt my head to keep the phone dry. "I'm busy, Dougy. I've got things to do. I don't have time to come down there."

"You can put off whatever asinine project

277

you're working on. We know about the toys you've handed out."

"It's Christmas next week. So I volunteered to hand out presents. What's the big deal?"

Dougy's snort makes it known that he doesn't believe me. "When did you get to be so charitable?"

I settle into the car and stare out the windshield. I don't see anyone in the parking lot who might be watching me, but I'm sure Dougy still has someone out there. He always backs off when I ask him to, but only for a little while. Inspector Douglas has the same complex as a jilted lover. It's always just a matter of time before he starts to get curious about what has become of me.

"Giving stuff away makes me feel good. Helps me to remember that there are people out there who aren't completely fucked in the head. You should try it sometime."

"I don't think the kids would be as excited about their presents if they knew that Santa Claus is the spawn of Orville Roberts."

"What are you going to do, Dougy? If I don't come down there to help you, will you out me to the public?" I sigh. "Just think of all the paperwork you'll have to fill out."

"Witness Protection is a pain in the ass."

I think about the false library card pressed into my back pocket. "Tell me about it."

There is a long pause before Dougy finally speaks. "I'm not going to out you. You're right, I don't want to have you moved again and there's no point in upsetting kids a week before Christmas. Although I'm sure your old girlfriend would love to break the story."

I haven't thought about Elsie in weeks. Dougy's mention of her makes my stomach churn. "If you ever go to the media with anything about me, you'd better give the story to someone else."

A chuckle fills my ear. "If you ever give me anything worth going to the news over, I promise. I'll find some other chump to report it."

I see a dark car pull into the lot. It isn't someone from Dougy's office unless he's gotten smart enough to have puttering old women be his lookouts. I consider getting out and offering to help the lady with her bags but the feeling of charity passes by the time she's loaded up her walker with groceries.

"I've got to go," I finally say.

Dougy grunts. "Of course you do. If you change your mind, let me know and I'll pick you up for visitation."

"Have a Merry Christmas, Dougy."

"Yeah. You too."

## Checked Out

I stare at the monitor in front of me. The library is busy with kids who are out of school for winter break. I've run out of ways to pretend I'm casually surfing the internet as I wait for the users of the computers on either side of me to vacate. My time at the keyboard is almost up and then I'm going to have to get back on the waiting list.

With five minutes to spare, I finally have my opening. The kid on my left leaves and the young woman on my right asks me to watch her bag while she goes to the bathroom. As soon as they are both out of sight I work furiously to drill down into the computer's security settings to disable the block that prevents users from downloading content.

Before the woman comes back to the computer beside me I've installed an incognito browser and buried the icon. I won't be able to take advantage of the untraceable search tool now, but when my name is called from the waiting list again it will be here. How I'll make sure to get back on this same computer, I don't know. I'll cross that bridge when I get there.

The librarian touches my shoulder and lets me know that it is time to give up my seat. Her tired face is surrounded by a wild halo of stringy hair. I watch her go back to the desk at the head of the computer area. She has buried her nose in a book before she's even sat down.

I take casual strides across the room to the sign up list laying at the edge of the librarian's desk and put my name down at the bottom of the page. "Hey, do you know how long the wait will be for another computer?"

The woman's eyes flick over the edge of her book at me. "One minute, please." She finishes reading the page she's on and puts the book down with a sigh before she picks up the clip board. She wears one of the most hideous holiday themed sweaters I've ever seen and I wonder if she is the type of person to have gotten swept up in the Ugly Sweater craze of hip professionals, or if it's the type of shirt that she normally wears.

She licks her lips and counts the names in silence. Her mouth twitches with each name that she reads. I decide that if she put any effort into un-frumping her clothes and did something with her hair that she would probably be pretty. She raises an untrimmed eyebrow at me and I realize that it's not likely to happen.

"It's going to be a couple of hours." She looks at the bank of computers and I follow her gaze to the seat that I just vacated which hasn't yet been filled. "Unless a few people don't check in for their turn."

As if on cue, a homeless looking teenager enters and heads our way. He grabs the list from the librarian and scrawls a signature beside his name. He may look as though he's just come in from a long day of standing on the corner with his hand out, but he smells like cinnamon and pine needles. He smiles at us briefly before he goes to claim the vacant computer and flashes straight white teeth that practically glow.

The woman behind the desk picks up her book again. Before she loses herself within the pages bound by a cover with a bare-chested man and curvy title letters she snaps, "It doesn't happen often. Just come back in an hour to see what's available."

A frustrated sigh escapes me. The sound seems to annoy the librarian who slides a bookmark into the book and roughly tosses it down on the desk. "Is there something else I can help you with?"

"Maybe. I need to do some research on poison. I wasn't able to find much useful information on the computer. Any chance you've got some books about that here?"

The librarian's dull face shifts. Her cheeks blush slightly and the corners of her mouth turn up.

283

"Sure we do. Come with me."

I nod and follow her. I'm overwhelmed with sudden self consciousness so I drop behind her a few paces. She notices the change in my stride and slows her gait to wait for me. Her smile radiates excitement when she turns to look at me and I don't know how to handle the change in her demeanor. "Sorry for lagging behind."

"Don't worry about it. So why are you interested in the craft of poison?" She walks beside me now, gesturing with her hand when we come to a set of shelves where we need to turn.

My brain flickers back to my notes about Neil Apollo. "I'm putting together a talk for some high school kids and need to find a way to make it more exciting. Most kids think chemical reactions are pretty boring. My colleagues and I are on a mission to find a topic that will pique their interest."

She tucks a clump of hair behind her ear and smiles. "Very cool." We reach a long row of shelves that bow under the weight of hundreds of thick books. The librarian traces her fingers along their spines until we reach the end of the section and then she opens her arms as if she might hug the shelf. "Here is the place to start. There are books on various toxins, both natural and synthetic."

I try to feign some confidence. "Have any favorites?"

The librarian's putrid green sweater wiggles across her chest when she leans down. She reaches for a thick book with pictures of mushrooms on the cover. "Of course I do."

"Wow. You didn't even have to think about that. Should I be worried?" I cross my arms and take a step back as if the book might kill me if I touch it. She laughs.

"I write Victorian era murder mysteries. Everyone who writes that time period seems to use arsenic to kill their victims. It helps to know that there were other things in that era that could kill you." She bounces on the balls of her feet with sudden giddiness. "Keeps the readers coming back for more."

"Creepy."

"Yeah." She laughs and extends the book out to me. "I'm Laura. Let me know if you have any other questions."

"I'll be sure to do that." I take the book from her and watch her skirt sway around her boot laced ankles when she darts out of the aisle and back to the computer lab. I pull a few more books off of the shelf and pile them up on a table at the end of the row. I set a timer on my phone to remind me to check back into the computer lab in an hour and begin to pour over the pages.

Of course taking care of Glen won't be as simple as getting him to take a dose of arsenic like the characters in some Victorian murder mystery. I read through my alarm going off, submerged in a book about over the counter poisons that have long ago been banned from consumer use. The topic is so engrossing that I take the entire stack of books with me back to the computer lab, unable to part with any of them even though they seem to weigh a thousand pounds.

I check in at Laura's desk to see how the wait for the computers is coming. Someone has scratched out the order of the list and has renumbered it so that I am next in line. She mouths words at me with an innocent look in her eye. "For the kids."

We share silent smiles while I wait for the people packing up their bags to vacate. The good smelling homeless kid who took my seat is among them and I jockey for position, ready to pounce the second he moves away from the computer. He nods and smiles at me when he pulls on his jacket, which I notice has holes ripped in strategic places. The holes are careful to not impede his access to his pockets and the area around each hole is machine stitched to prevent it from fraying further than its intended placement. It occurs to me that the kid probably paid good money for the jacket and is actually trying to achieve the hobo look on purpose.

His scent lingers in the small cubicle surrounding the computer and I shake my head. I don't understand people. I wave one of the smaller books through the air to disperse the fragrance, then deposit the entire stack I'm carrying onto the tiny desk. When Laura has her nose replanted in her romance novel and it seems the people on either side of me are absorbed in their respective Facebook pages, I click on the incognito web browser.

While I would love to simply buy a case of toxic powder to dump on Glen's head, I'm having trouble finding a way to buy anything that would take him out. I think back to when I was a kid and there was a big Tylenol scare. I look up the Time Magazine article on the poisonings and try to figure out how the tax consultant that was suspected for the poisonings might have gotten a hold of enough potassium cyanide to kill all those people.

If I were really someone who taught science,

like the Neil Apollo persona stamped on my library card, I'd already know all of these answers. I'm sure that real science teachers have access to all kinds of chemicals and compounds to use for educational purposes. I look up science lab supply catalogs online and scroll through dozens of pages that list all of the chemicals I could ever hope for. Each page is embellished with giant red letters.

*This product will be shipped to a school or industrial business address only. Don't even think about trying to ship this to your apartment, dumbass.*

I consider creating a laboratory company. I could rent a small warehouse and have the chemicals shipped there. Maybe I could pull it off, but it would take a while to pull together. Not to mention that starting an entire company just to take care of Glen screams "premeditation" if anyone found out what I was doing. Besides, I really doubt that I could get something of that magnitude done with Dougy tailing me.

I glance at the pile of books on the desk. The one that Laura first suggested is suddenly more interesting. I Google "poisonous mushrooms of the Northwest" and am bombarded with thousands of pages of mushroom identification sites. It doesn't take

288

long for me to find stories of people who have been accidentally poisoned when mushrooming in Oregon.

I close out the incognito browser and sift through the books on my desk. I pull three volumes that have sections on the toxicity of mushrooms and stack them on top of the book Laura selected. I put all of the other books on a returns cart. I gather up the stuff I want to take home and stop by Laura's desk on the way out.

"Hey, thanks for the help." I whisper.

She winks at me from behind her book. "Anytime."

## Tailed

I don't notice the black Suburban following me until I've passed the last exit for Salem. At first I think it's just another guy headed south on a sunny winter afternoon, but when I test the theory by pulling into the slow lane and dropping my speed so that he'll pass, he follows suit. I realize that I saw the same Suburban about a half an hour ago. He must have been doing a good job of keeping a few cars between us until now. Whatever cover he was using has been lost now that most of the traffic has pulled into the city. The further we get from Salem, the less there is for him to hide behind.

There comes a point when you get so used to being tailed by cops that that it doesn't scare you any more. Instead, you stare into your rearview mirror and comment to yourself about all of the stupid things they do when they're trying to be incognito. For example, driving a giant blacked out Suburban. Don't they realize that if they really want to blend into the Oregon countryside that they should plod along in a vintage Volvo station wagon or a Subaru with a bicycle on the roof rack?

I flick on my hazards and pull over to the

shoulder. Despite the sun that streams through the car windows, a blast of frozen air assaults me when I open the door. I fiddle around in the car for a minute, keeping my eye on the mirror to see what the Suburban does. Its driver has pulled over as well, and I see the guy behind the wheel hurriedly putting on a dirty plaid trucker's jacket and a tattered baseball cap. Because that'll convince me he's just a regular dude pulling over to help.

I get the rest of the way out of the car and make my way back to the trunk. I pop it open, then move to lean over the side of the car so that my back isn't fully facing the Suburban. I keep an eye on the guy getting out of the rig as I pull out my emergency tool kit and dig around to find my tire pressure gauge.

"Hey there," the guy says as he approaches. "Car trouble?"

"Yeah, she's pulling to the right a little so I thought I'd check to make sure I don't have a leak." I wiggle the found tire pressure gauge at him and then play at checking the air in my rear tires.

"It sucks having tire problems when it's this cold out." The guy's smile gleams from between freshly shaven cheeks. "Have you been out here long?"

"Oh, boy. Yeah." I pull the sleeve of my jacket

up and check my watch. "It must have been a whole four seconds before I noticed you pull over. I really don't know what I would have done if you hadn't stopped. Would have had to wait for your backup to arrive, I guess."

The guy puffs his chest as though he's about to play at being offended, then realizes he's been made and takes the hat off. "Well, if you're having trouble, you may as well let me help."

I toss the tire gauge into the trunk and slam the lid. "You know what would help?"

"What's that?"

"If you would tell Inspector Douglas to give you the rest of the day off. Then go the fuck back to wherever you came from and leave me the hell alone."

"Calm down. There's no need to cuss me out. You know I can't leave you, Peter."

"Why not? Are you afraid that it might affect your next annual review if you don't file a report that you followed me into the woods and watched me take a hike?"

The guy puts his hands on his hips and scowls. "Is that what you're doing?"

I look up into the sky, exasperated. "For fuck's sake, yes."

"You're a long way from home to go for a hike. There are perfectly good places to hike right by your apartment."

I wish I could punch the guy in the face, but assaulting an officer probably won't get me anywhere. "I've seen all of those trails. I'm just taking a day trip to explore the woods further south."

"How do I know that you're not running?"

I hope that the daggers in my eyes are as piercing as I intend them to be. I pick up a foot and wiggle it at him. "I'm wearing hiking boots." I move to the side of the car and pull out my backpack. I unzip it and dump the contents on my trunk. "I've got a trail map for the Rogue River-Siskiyou National Forest and a sack lunch."

The guy appears to doubt his own words when he says, "You could be trying to play us."

"I've got fifty bucks in my wallet and didn't bring a sleeping bag. I promise, I'll be back home before midnight."

"I can't just let you go. I've got a job to do."

I know that he is coming with me no matter what I do. "What's your name?"

"Inspector Smith." He nods with the curt introduction.

293

"I'm not calling you 'Inspector', unless you want your title to be followed by 'Gadget'."

His eyes narrow. "Just call me Smith."

"Fine, Smith." The keys in my hand jingle involuntarily. "If you're coming along, how about we do the environment a favor and carpool? That way you don't look like such a giant douchewhistle and I don't have to listen to my Navigation system bark at me every thirty feet."

Smith turns to look at the gleaming bulk of the Suburban and shrugs. "I suppose there's no reason to keep my distance."

I nod to him and then move to get back in my car. "Follow me to the next rest stop. We'll dump your rig there."

# Company

"Have you ever gone mushroom hunting before?"

Smith doesn't look at me. Instead, he stares at the tiny map on my cell phone screen. He's trying to figure out how far the quarter inch strip of highway is in real life so we know where to make our next turn. A minute passes and he must have figured out the distance conversion because he sets my phone down in the cup holder between us. "No. I hate mushrooms."

I shake my head. "It's a shame. They're some of the best treats that nature has to offer."

We have ridden most of the way in silence. He picks up the phone and fiddles with the navigation every few minutes. Once in a while he'll make a comment on how much further we have to drive to hit the spot I've picked out. Mostly, we just stare at the road ahead.

The yellow lines wink at me as my car chews up the asphalt. The sun forces its warmth through the glass of the windshield. It is one of those road trips through Oregon that makes a person realize that there is nowhere else they'd rather be. The ground is unseasonably dry and the trees wave their green

295

branches as if they are inviting us out for a walk. Everything about today is perfect, except for Smith.

As excited as I was when I started on this trip, I still have no idea what I'm doing. My chances of success were slim to begin with, and now I wonder how I'll pull it off with a U.S. Marshal looking over my shoulder.

We reach the turnoff that we've been waiting for. I pull the car over onto a thin layer of gravel tossed down on a level patch of ground and park directly beneath a sign that announces the trailhead. I get out of the car and rummage through the back seat and trunk, collecting my backpack and making sure to grab the book that lists edible mushrooms and their poisonous copycats.

I'm ready to go, but Smith hasn't moved from the passenger seat. I lean against the car and he props his door open just wide enough to talk to me.

"You're really going in there?" Smith nods towards the woods. He's abandoned the heavy plaid jacket that he wore when we were pulled over on I-5 and I can see him shiver when a cold breeze whispers at us.

"Aren't you?" I adjust the backpack on my shoulders and flash him a smile.

296

"I'm wearing dress shoes." He drops a foot below the door to show me, and the lines on his face darken when he frowns.

"What is it that they say in the Boy Scouts? *Dress to survive, not to arrive.*" I tilt my head toward Smith's dangling foot. "You might want to work on that."

Smith glares at me. He grabs the plaid jacket and trucker cap from before. He slams my car door harder than necessary, then marches up the trail into the woods.

I push ahead and Smith follows me with the enthusiasm of a reluctant prom date. We've hiked for an hour before I find anything resembling a mushroom. What I do find, the fungi identifier book I've brought along says are Hedgehogs. Perfectly edible. I pick the mushrooms carefully, storing them in my backpack. Smith continues ahead, bored with the discovery.

I meet up with him at a fork in the trail and when he turns to me, his face is set with dissatisfaction. I suggest we head down the northern route and soon we find a ring of red capped mushrooms beneath a pine tree. I flip open the book to identify them.

"You seriously came all this way to find mushrooms." It isn't a question. More of a statement that Smith has just realized that this is all I'm doing.

"Yes." The mushrooms are listed as being potentially poisonous, but more likely something that will produce a bad psychedelic trip. I kneel down beside them and pull a pocket notebook out and jot down the details of the discovery. When I'm finished, I look up at Smith. "It's a nice, quiet hobby. A lot of the ones you find can be eaten. Some of them, not so much."

Smith nods, then shuffles his feet in the dirt. "How long do you think we'll be out here?"

I check the time on my phone. "It'll be daylight for another four hours."

We move further down the trail. I trip a couple of times, looking intently at the forest on either side of the trail and missing tree roots that have risen up in the dirt. The quietness of the woods would be relaxing if it weren't interrupted by Smith's tired sighs every couple of minutes. I try to engage him. "What do you do in your down time? You know, for fun."

Smith shrugs his shoulders. "I like to go to the gym."

I nod. His love for the weight machines is visible. "Anything else?"

"I'm a remote member of the C.C.I.R.I." Smith

almost blushes in response to my blank stare. "Cold Case Investigative Research Institute. We collaborate to solve famous cold cases. Our group is based in Atlanta, but we're working the Kyron Horman case this year so I've been busier with it than normal."

"So when you're on the clock you do physical training and look for people, and when you have down time you go to the gym and try to solve missing persons cases? You've got a lot of depth, Smith."

A fallen tree off the trail catches my eye and I'm into the woods before Smith can process my comment. The tree fell long ago and has started to rot in several spots. I flip through the mushroom book and find what I'm looking for. I pull some latex gloves and a plastic bag out of my backpack and I've collected a dozen of the generic looking brown mushrooms before Smith has gotten curious enough to follow me. By the time he reaches me, the gloves and baggie have been tucked away and I'm writing in my notebook.

"Now what did you find?" Smith kneels down beside me and squints at the log.

"Galerina marginata. They look pretty similar to your average mushroom, don't they?" Smith nods as he leans over my shoulder to see what I'm writing. I'm just writing down the location of the fungus, so I don't

299

do anything to hide the paper from him. "That's why they're so dangerous. These little brown mushrooms might be edible, but they also might be poisonous."

"How can you tell the difference?" Smith rocks back on his heels, putting some distance between himself and the offending fungus.

"Shape of the gills, spore print, coloration." I pretend that I know what I'm talking about, but am just parroting something I read. I consider that he may have seen me picking them and offer, "I took a couple of samples. I'm going to do some more research back home."

"Wouldn't it be safer to just get your mushrooms at the grocery store?" Smith follows when I get up and we pick our way back to the trail.

"It is." I shrug. "But where's the fun in picking mushrooms out of Styrofoam wrapped in plastic?"

# Processing

A dozen plastic bags are spread out across my dining room table. I have three fungus identification books open beside them and I busy myself with cross-identifying the mushrooms from my haul. I toss anything that looks to be edible or only mildly irritating to the stomach in the trash. If I ever bump into Smith again I'll have to play up how well they might have gone in a stir fry, but the truth is that I'm not a big fan of eating mushrooms, either.

I'm left with three bags of mushrooms that will probably mimic food poisoning, but end in death. I skim over the details of the fatal symptoms on each mushroom. The little I've read about dying from any species of mushroom is horrific, so I decide to spare myself any extraneous details. I've come so far that I can't let the graphic description of kidney failure talk me out of it now.

My appointment with Glen is tomorrow afternoon. I don gloves when I pull a couple of mushrooms out of each bag and lay them out to dry. I put the tray in the oven to speed up the process and then dump the leftover fresh mushrooms into the trash.

While I wait on the mushrooms to dry, I dig

out the sheet of paper with Glen's name and address on it. I palm the AA phone in my hand and wonder if talking to him will ruin my plan. Maybe he'll be pleasant today. Make me decide to just give him the electric guitar and be done with it. The phone rings a dozen times. I'm about to hang up when the line connects.

"Yeah?" Glen's voice is hoarse.

"Hi Glen. It's Ted from Alphabet Apes. I'm calling to confirm our appointment for tomorrow." I slide my appointment book toward me and flip it open. His name glares up at me from the otherwise empty page.

"Did you figure out what I won?"

"I won't know until you bring that winning box into the office. You still have it, don't you?"

A part of me hopes that Glen will tell me that he didn't really have a box to begin with. I'm overwhelmed with anxiety and elation when he says, "Yeah. I've got it right here."

I clear my throat. "Great. I look forward to scanning it so we can see what you've won."

"Did you get anything with the Alphabet Apes logo?"

My lips purse and I feel my whole body tense.

302

Even when I hope that Glen will give me an out, he focuses on getting something he can sell for a profit. "A few things. Maybe you'll get lucky."

Glen grunts. "I hope so. The price on my crossbow jumped two hundred dollars over the weekend. I've got to flip this shit before it's totally out of my reach."

"Used by Derrick something?"

"Daryl Dixon," Glen corrects.

"Right. From that zombie show."

Glen's disgust at my ignorance is palatable. "It's more than just a show. It's a fictional documentation of a sociological reboot brought on by mass viral plague. The characters' resilience is not only plausible, but the storyline is probable should such an event occur in present day."

My eyes roll. "Maybe I will check it out sometime."

"With the present state of the world's bio warfare capabilities, I suggest that you do. Unless you don't mind becoming a mindless drone who eats your neighbors."

"I'll see you tomorrow, Glen." I hang up the phone.

After checking the mushrooms, I putter

through the apartment. I collect all of the boxes of cereal that I've been using for the prize displays into a stack. I have more Alphabet Apes than I thought. Thirty boxes stand in a line across my kitchen counter. I pull my vacuum sealer out of the cabinet and set it up on the table.

I open one of the boxes, careful to not tear the cardboard tabs so that I can glue them back together later. The plastic sleeve full of cereal slides easily from the box. I use a straight edge and a hobby knife to slice the top open evenly.

Now all there is to do is wait for the mushrooms to finish drying. I'll pound them into a powder and mix the compound into the cereal before resealing the bag and doing my best to make the box look as though it just came from the factory.

# Grand Prize

The flutter of butterflies drums in my stomach when I set up the prizes at the rented office. I haven't set any other appointments up this week. Not only am I nervous about giving Glen his prize, but it's also Christmas Eve and despite the amount of prizes I have left to distribute, there simply haven't been many calls from potential winners. The few people I have heard from are busy with plans for Christmas and New Year's so it seems like an appropriate time to take a break.

I stack a pyramid of cereal boxes in the corner of the room. The box I tampered with sits front and center. It looks almost identical to the rest of the boxes, but a small crease on a corner of the top flap of the box announces its presence at me. I try to convince myself that the difference isn't substantial enough to turn Glen off of opening it. I suppose only time will tell.

The intercom beeps and the receptionist announces Glen's arrival. It doesn't take long before he's standing in the doorway. A flattened cereal box is tucked under his sweaty arm.

"You made it." I force a wide smile and reach my hand out to shake his. He doesn't return the gesture, instead slides in the room past me and sits down beside the laptop and bar code scanner.

"Let's figure this shit out."

"OK." I squirm through the narrow gap that he's left behind his chair and tap the keypad to wake the laptop from its sleep. "Pretty exciting, isn't it?"

"I'm trembling in my boots."

I can feel my smile fall, but I push it out again in my best attempt at salesman enthusiasm. "May I see your box please?"

The cardboard is tattered and has heavy creases across the middle. It looks as though it was folded down to fit in a manila envelope. I glance sideways at Glen and wonder if he cares that I make the connection between the folds and his obsession with eBay. "Where did you say you bought this?"

Glen stares me in the eye, defiant. "Does it matter?"

My rage boils beneath my skin and I wish I could just reach over and wrap my hands around his flabby throat. I fantasize about pressing the life out of him, watching his blotchy skin depress in long rows beneath my fingers. His eyes would bulge, glassy and bloodshot as he struggled for breath. He would flail against me in a battle of wills before falling limp in his chair.

But how would I ever drag his fat ass out of the office without anyone noticing?

"It doesn't really matter where you bought the cereal," I state. "We just use the information to track which stores have the highest redemption rate for future promotional opportunities."

Glen shrugs. "If it doesn't matter, then scan it."

I pass the UPC code under the red light of the scanner, and my computer beeps appropriately. The programmed macro responds and a window opens. Text scrolls across the window.

*Congratulations! You've won the Alphabet Apes grand prize for Portland, Oregon.*

Glen's face stretches into an odd grimace. It takes me a moment to realize that he's smiling. He leans forward, perched on the edge of his seat. His fingers tap the table nervously as he takes a slow look around the room. "So, what's the grand prize?"

I gesture through the collection of prizes toward the pyramid of cereal. I clap him on the back with my other hand. "You, Sir, have won a year supply of Alphabet Apes cereal."

Glen's smile falls. "What?"

I get up from my chair and dance around the conference table. The yellow cereal boxes almost glow under the fluorescent overhead lights. I pat the bent corner of the tainted box when I reach it. With the crumpled disrepair of the box Glen brought in, there's no way that he'll think anything of a small depression in the cardboard.

I pick up a couple of the boxes and wave them in the air toward Glen. "You've won a year's supply. Fifty-two boxes of delicious Alphabet Apes cereal! Of course, we want to make sure that you enjoy the boxes when they're fresh, so you will receive twenty boxes now. Thirty two more will be delivered to you in about five months."

Glen slouches against the back of his chair. Disappointment radiates from his side of the room. He eyeballs a stack of gift cards. "Can I trade the grand prize for something else?"

I shake my head. I lift my hands in a "what can I do" motion and do my best to look sympathetic. "Oh, no. Prizes are non-transferable. Only one prize per household."

I sit back down with Glen and fill out the simple prize redemption form that I have on hand. It doesn't include much more than his name and the address he wants the rest of his cereal boxes delivered to. When we are done, I make a couple of trips to load

308

the boxes of cereal that represent his first installment into his car. Glen doesn't help.

"At least my grocery bill will be smaller," Glen finally says as I stack the last few boxes in his back seat.

"Absolutely. One whole meal a day that you won't have to worry about for a while." The happiness that I exude is genuine. I made sure that the tainted box is on top of the stack, easy for him to access. I imagine him placing it front and center in his kitchen cabinet. I look away when I realize that I'm staring at him expectantly.

"Well thanks, I guess." Glen shuffles around the car to the driver's door.

"Merry Christmas. Maybe Santa will bring you that crossbow." I wink at him over the roof of the car.

"Christmas implies religious connotations. I prefer Happy Holidays. It's more inclusive." Glen pulls the door open and slumps into the car.

I take a few steps back until I am even with the curb. "Happy Holidays," I mutter when the car door shuts and the engine revs. It certainly feels like a holiday worth celebrating when he pulls out of the parking lot.

# Resolutions

Jeanne's smile brightens the otherwise gloomy day. Dark clouds have hovered overhead since Christmas. Now it is nearly mid-January and the entire city seems sleepy and unsettled. It was harder for me to book this appointment with Jeanne than it has ever been. I guess seasonal depression translates into a busy schedule for therapists.

"How were your holidays?" Jeanne holds a new pen. I wonder if it was a Christmas present from another client, or something she picked up for herself.

"They were great. Honestly, probably the best I've ever had." I smile at her and she beams back at me.

"Did you do anything special?"

I nod. "I delivered Christmas baskets. It was fun. Very personally rewarding."

"The volunteering bug has really bitten you, hasn't it?" Jeanne marks the page with notes about my giving spirit. I'm sure she finds the trait endearing. Attractive.

"It really makes you feel good, you know?" We share a meaningful look.

"Yes. We volunteer at a homeless shelter the day after Christmas every year. Most people want to volunteer on Christmas Day, but we want to make people feel cared for a little longer."

"We?" I glance down at Jeanne's fingers and don't see a ring.

"My girlfriend and I." Her moist lips rise into a smile and I imagine them caressing the naked skin of another woman.

"You mean your good friend, who happens to be a woman?"

Jeanne giggles. It is a tiny, conspiring laugh that indicates we are sharing an intimate secret. I try to imagine holding her, but even in my mind she slips away from me. I gaze down at her stocking clad legs and can see them clamped around the body of another gorgeous woman. Jeanne runs her fingers through the strange woman's hair. Jeanne guides the woman's face down between her knees, then the two of them scramble against the fabric of Jeanne's skirt. They are heated, panting. I am so disgusted that I have to look away.

I remember my father telling me about the horrors of homosexuality when I was a kid. I never understood what harm it could cause. My father interpreted scriptures that showed how the sins they committed brought down entire civilizations. I've thought that he was wrong all of these years. But now in this space with Jeanne, the intimate moments we've shared tainted with this new rejection of my sex, I find that the acid in my stomach gurgles and I have to cover my mouth to keep from retching.

I come back to reality when Jeanne's hand touches my knee. "Peter, are you all right?"

The touch of her dirty hand makes my skin crawl. I pull my knee away from her, but I can already feel the sin dripping through the fabric. I can't look at her. I can only mumble, "You are an adulteress. An abomination."

Jeanne sits upright in her chair. She is flustered and confused. "Come on Peter. I thought we were friends. Surely my sexual orientation doesn't matter."

I steel myself against the nausea rising up in my gut and look up at her. Where a beautiful woman once sat, there is now a degraded slut. Her rosy cheeks have faded, her soft skin has congealed. Her unfaithfulness to my love is revolting to every one of my senses. "How can you possibly advise people coming to you for help when you are living a life of outright sin?"

"I think you're being a little unfair." Jeanne caps her pen and sets it on the table. Her fingers graze the shaft of the pen and I can see her ramming it into her girlfriend. When the light catches the chrome accents I can almost see the vaginal residue dried to them.

"God is going to punish you for your immorality." I rise from my chair. I pull my sleeve down around my hand before I touch the door. Jeanne's infidelity is like a disease creeping through the room.

Jeanne looks away from me, her demeanor exuding shame. Her eyes water and her voice trembles when she states, "I think it would be best for you to find a more conservative therapist."

I give a curt nod and shut the door behind me.

# Office Work

My arms stretch above my head. I roll to my side and let my eyes flutter open. I've had the same dream a dozen times now. Glen pours a bowl of cereal from a box with a bent flap. The cereal tastes funny, but he pushes past the unfamiliar taste and finishes the bowl. It was free, after all.

Time speeds forward, and Glen is crouched over a toilet. He suspects food poisoning. But what has he eaten? It must have come from some bad sushi. Or maybe a pizza with unfamiliar toppings. After a while he starts to feel better. He checks his eBay listings. Calculates the funds in his Paypal account and compares them to the cost of a crossbow.

Weeks later a neighbor notices a strange smell coming from the house. No one has seen or heard from Glen in a long time. No one answers when they knock on the door. They call the police for a wellness check. The police find him slumped against his desk. His hands are still splayed across the keyboard. He was trolling some poor teenager on a forum when he died.

A relaxed sigh whooshes through my nostrils. I lay on my back with my hands tucked under my head and I stare at the ceiling. It has been a month since

Glen picked up his grand prize. He might have eaten the cereal by now. The mushroom's toxins may already be coursing through his system. Perhaps he has a stomach ache. Maybe he's already dead.

I roll out of bed and start to get ready for work. After breaking up with Jeanne I count my blessings that I haven't been contacted by Dad or Dougy again. I can't handle the drama of these toxic people in my life any more. I'm determined for things to go back to as close to normal as possible, aside from waiting for Glen to die.

My boss seemed surprised to hear from me. There had been some minor co-ordination to get me back on the schedule rotation and I spent a few days easing back into the monotony of office work. Then came a new project assignment and quickly it was as if I'd never left.

Today marks my third week back at work. No one, not even the lady in Human Resources, asked me about my leave. I am surprised when I walk through the campus to my office and Jeff, an engineer I only have intermittent work history with, stops to ask how I am.

"I heard that your dad was battling some kind of cancer. Who won the fight?" Jeff abandons whatever course he was on and matches his stride to mine.

315

"I guess you'd say my dad won." I look at Jeff sideways. "For now, anyway."

"That's great!" Jeff pounds me on the back in congratulations. "How is he recovering?"

"I'm not sure. We aren't speaking."

Jeff skips a step in shock, then jogs forward until his pace is once again even with mine. "That's rough. It's good you were there for him. I lost my dad to cancer a few years ago. It's a lot to go through."

"I'm sorry for your loss," I offer.

Jeff claps me on the back again. "Well I hope you two are able to patch things up. What's the point on getting a second lease on life if you've got to live it without your family?"

"Sometimes family is more of a curse than a blessing."

He snorts. "Don't I know it. That's how I feel about my wife some days. So how are things going now that you're back at work?"

"You're the first person to ask me that." We share an awkward glance. "It's okay. I picked up a couple of new hobbies while I was out. It's helping to balance the stress."

"Sounds like you did a lot of growing while you were away." Jeff grabs me by the elbow and pulls me to a stop. "I've got to run to a meeting. It was great to see you. Let me know if you ever need anything."

We shake hands and Jeff turns away from me. He walks quickly back the way we came. The exchange stays on my mind long after Jeff is gone. I think about Dad and his offer to give up more bodies as I boot up my computer and skim through obituaries online, looking for Glen's name. I wonder if Dad had ever poisoned anyone. I try to imagine him pouring over a dozen newspapers, eagerly searching for proof of his handiwork. I can't see him pawing through the news like I am. Dad is blunt, and I doubt it ever took anyone long to realize that he was going to be the last person they'd meet.

But maybe he had. Maybe he'd know how it feels to go through the motions while waiting to find out how long his victim would drag things out before finally succumbing to their inevitable end.

## Salem

I smile at Dad when he enters the visitation room. He takes his time joining me in the corner, a glare of discontent filling the distance between us. When he finally sits, he breaks his stare and looks down at his hands.

"Sorry it's been so long," I mumble. "I had to work through my anger."

"You abandoned me."

My gaze drops to Dad's hands. His fingers are slimmer than I remember. The skin is raw, small cracks trailing between the creases of his joints. He subconsciously picks at a callused sore on his left hand. I reach forward to touch him, but he recoils and pushes his hands into his lap.

"I'm sorry. I reacted poorly when I found out about the roofies. We can't change what happened when I was a kid. All we can do now is apologize to one another and cherish the time we have left."

Dad looks up. "I accept your apology."

I lean forward, eager to hear him say that he is sorry for not being there for me when I was growing up. I hope he will say that he wishes he was a better parent. Ache for him to tell me that he never meant to hurt me.

All he does is smile at me, content with my remorse.

"Do you have anything to say to me?" I am so far on the edge of my seat that if I move another inch, I'll fall.

"There are three bodies stored in barrels in a warehouse in Salem."

The lack of apology comes like a slap to the face. I slide back in my chair, the moment of hopeful anticipation ruined by Dad's self absorbed confession. I slump with disappointment against the hard steel and wave to someone in a corrections uniform. The man comes over to our table and leans so close to me that I can feel his breath on my cheek.

"Call Inspector Douglas. Tell him we're going to Salem." The corrections officer nods and disappears to make the call. I stare at Dad, who looks incredibly pleased with himself. With a lifetime of practice, I push past the pain of being unworthy of Dad's apology. I take a deep breath and shift my focus. "Who are they?"

Dad's smile widens. "Runaways. I collected them in the summer of '72. No one ever came looking for them."

I pinch my nose in frustration. "How on earth could you keep barrels with bodies hidden this long?"

A laugh rolls through the air between us.

"Warehouse managers don't much care what you store as long as the rent is paid on time. Getting a monthly payment to them took some doing at first, but when they invented auto-draft, it got really easy."

"You've been paying rent on warehouse space for over forty years? How the hell can you afford that?"

Dad shrugs. "It's called budgeting, Hen."

## Pansy

Dad and I stand at the mouth of a gaping warehouse. The wind crashes against the metal building and even the officers inside have to stand close to one another to hear what one another are saying. Dad puffs on a cigarette, careful to cup the paper in his hand so that the embers aren't blown away before he finishes.

"How is your project going?" Smoke leaves his mouth with each word spoken. It vanishes on the wind in an instant, but the smell somehow still lingers between us.

I smile for the first time today. "It's done."

Dad's eyes light up and he rubs his shoulder against mine in congratulations. "I didn't think you'd be able to pull it off."

My laugh is whisked away on the wind. A marshal a dozen feet away from me looks over at us casually, but he doesn't appear to have heard what we've said. "I wasn't going to do it. But this guy showed up and I knew he was the one."

"I told you that is how it would be. It's as if they have been searching for you, isn't it?"

I shake my head. "Not exactly. He isn't miserable or anything. He's just an asshole."

"You mean he *was* an asshole." Dad grins. I shrug. "You did say that the project was done. He's dead, right?"

"I'm not sure." I look down at my feet, suddenly conscious of the way the loops of my white laces drag in the wet gravel.

"What did you do?"

"I had the contest, the one we talked about. This guy Glen came in, a real piece of work. I gave him the grand prize."

"What was the grand prize? Strangulation? A dirty needle? A bullet to the head?"

I shake my head. "Poisoned cereal."

"You forced him to eat poisoned cereal, and you don't know if he died?" Dad's brow furrows. "Did you get the mix wrong?"

"I loaded it into his car, so I know he took it with him. But he hasn't shown up in the obituaries yet."

Dad tosses his cigarette on the ground and rubs his face with his hands. "What were you hoping – that he'd move in with you so that you could make sure he'd eat it?"

"No." My answer comes out so weak that even I can't hear it with the wind howling in my ears. I set my shoulders and force my chin up to hide my embarrassment. "I wanted to make sure it looked like an accident. The longer it takes for him to eat it, the less of a chance there is that anyone will connect him to me."

"And if he never eats it, then you're definitely in the clear."

"He'll eat it. It was free cereal. He said that he was glad he'd have a smaller grocery bill."

Dad shakes his head. "It's sloppy. I don't like it."

"It's okay." I perk up, trying to exude sincere enthusiasm. "It's like waiting to find out if I've won the lottery. Some day, I'm going to hit big."

Dad laughs at me. It makes me feel small. When he looks at me through his tear filled eyes I wonder if the wetness is from the bitter cold, or from the disappointment that his only son can't fulfill his one desire. "I think there's something you're missing about playing the lottery."

"What is that?"

"A fair amount of the time, nobody wins."

# Food Bank

Twelve weeks have passed, and still no hyped story on the news about the man who died of liver failure after eating a bowl of Alphabet Apes cereal. I've subscribed to six newspapers and check the obituaries every day. It doesn't matter which paper I flip through, I never find the satisfaction of Glen's puffy face looking up at me from the newsprint. I pick up my keys and head out the door. It's time to pay him a visit.

I drive through Glen's neighborhood at a crawl. Each house looks like it's in the running for the next Homeowners Association "Yard of the Month". Bushes trimmed precisely 3.5 feet high. Despite it being a cold winter day, each front yard has green grass without a blade out of place. I look down at Glen's address on the form on my lap to check the house number.

I pull around a bend in the road, and there he is. Glen rakes grass clippings in his front yard, oblivious to me driving by. He wears the same flannel shirt as the last time I saw him, a pair of metallic silver shorts and flip-flops despite the cold. At least the knee high black socks appear to be keeping his calves warm.

I pull to the curb a couple houses down and get out of my car. I can see him from where I stand, slowly pulling the leaves toward him into a neat pile. Someone calls to him from over the pristine white fence along his driveway, and he waves at them.

I check my car's side mirror to make sure I don't look as flustered as I feel. I push a shock of hair away from my forehead and straighten my collar before I walk toward him. I'm casual; pausing to look at a flower, smiling at a kid riding by on his bike. Just out for a walk. Off to see the man who should be dead.

I walk past Glen's yard and wait for him to recognize me. He smiles at me briefly as I pass but doesn't stop his work. I make it halfway past his driveway and stop. I turn, pretending to think for a moment and then force my best smile. "Glen? Glen Crookston?"

He looks up at me, confused but friendly. He smiles. "Yeah?"

"I thought that was you." I trot over to him and thrust my hand out to him for a handshake. When he grasps it, the heat that radiates from his skin makes me angry. Despite my disappointment at the pulse that throbs in his fingers as we shake hands I am able to keep the smile pasted on my face.

"I'm sorry, do I know you?"

"Ted Willard. From Alphabet Apes." I tuck my

fists under my arms and dance like a monkey as I sing, "When you want to feel great, try some Alphabet Apes!"

Glen's face relaxes into a more natural scowl. "Oh, that's right. You were the guy with the contest. That's been a couple months ago now, hasn't it?"

"Three months. How are you doing? And how is that mountain of cereal holding up?"

He chuckles. I hate the way his flabby skin jiggles with the effort. "Oh, man. The first couple of weeks all I did was eat cereal. But then, too much of a good thing, you know? Had to switch my breakfast up a bit."

"Really? Well. I hope you don't take too long of a break. Those Apes won't eat themselves, you know." I give Glen a wink. "Besides, that second shipment should turn up soon."

"Don't I know it. Well, between you and me, I just kind of got sick of them. They were doing a big food drive down at the church, so I donated the rest to them." Glen beams at the mention of his unusual moment of charity.

My stomach drops to my feet. "You did what?"

"Donated them. Man, there must have been fifteen boxes left by the time I was sick of them."

326

I look into Glen's eyes. All pretense of a jovial coincidence at our meeting is lost. "When did you do that, exactly?"

"I don't know. A month ago, I guess."

"And they still have the food down at the church?"

Glen's beard shifts when he shakes his head. "No. They sent it all off to a food bank somewhere. They said they collected five thousand pounds of food. Isn't that something?" His focus shifts and he looks at me a minute. "Ted, you aren't looking too good. Are you okay?"

"No, Glen. I am absolutely not okay." I draw back and punch him square in the mouth. We're both surprised by the strike. My knuckles throb in time with my racing heart.

Glen tilts off balance but catches himself with the rake to keep from falling into the leaves. He wags his jaw and massages it with his off hand to make sure it still works, then spits out a trickle of blood where his teeth have cut into his lips. "What the hell, man?"

"What part of 'prizes are non-transferable' do you not understand?"

# Bound

Glen's eyes follow me around the room. I've somehow managed the strength to tie him to his recliner and now I don't know what to do with him. I pace around his dim living room and try to decide what to do next. I leave him alone long enough to scrounge through his kitchen for something to eat and settle on cooking up a couple of personal pizzas in his toaster oven.

I go back to the living room and sit on the couch across from Glen with the pizzas on a plate on my lap. I nibble at one, but it's still too hot, so I set the plate down beside me to cool. I stare Glen in the eye. "Why the fuck didn't you just eat the cereal?"

Glen's eyes water and he whimpers beneath the tape over his mouth. His shoulders shake while he cries. I reach toward a stack of remotes on the coffee table and mash the buttons until the TV springs to life. I browse the channels while I think. I settle on the mid-day news, letting my mind mull over the sounds of stock failings and school fund-raising efforts.

The screen flashes and shows a reporter standing on the corner in Southeast Portland. His face is somber as he reports. "A Portland area man is the only survivor in what officials are claiming to be a domestic terror attack. A woman reported to be his girlfriend, and their two children, died tonight after what appears to be intentional food poisoning."

I turn the volume up and the pizzas fall to the floor when I grab the arm of the couch for support. The reporter takes a deep breath and continues. "Here is Lisa with details."

A woman standing in front of the hospital's emergency doors appears on the screen. "Thank you, Rob. I am here just outside of St. Vincent Hospital's ICU where Vincent White says he is lucky to be alive. He and his family picked up a box of food at the Oregon Food Bank on January fifteenth, the same way they have for the last six months following White's layoff. Everything seemed normal until the family returned home and prepared their first meal of the week."

A picture appears on the screen, showing a box of Alphabet Apes and an empty bowl. I glance over at Glen. He strains to see the television from his off-center angle, and his eyes go wide when he sees the box. I turn back to the screen.

"White states that approximately twenty-four hours after eating from a box of Alphabet Apes, a popular cereal that the children were excited to receive, the family each experienced symptoms of nausea, vomiting and diarrhea. He says that they didn't initially report the food poisoning because they regularly receive food near the end of its shelf life and they assumed it was the canned milk, and not the cereal, that caused the ill effects.

A photo of the family appears. A large black man, a petite white woman and two mocha colored children stand with arms linked in front of a grove of trees. Each has brilliant smiles. "It wasn't until three days later when the family again ate the cereal with fresh milk that they realized that the cereal itself may be the culprit. White says the he and girlfriend Susan Peters, a local student studying to be a nurse, contacted Alphabet Apes to report the bad box of cereal. Both times eating the cereal, the family's symptoms appeared to clear and the incident was attributed to food poisoning."

Lisa the reporter returns to the screen, now placed in front of the glowing Hospital sign. "Ten days after the initial meal, the symptoms returned. When the children became jaundiced, which is a yellowing of the skin and eyes, Peters and White took them to urgent care. It was determined that all four individuals were experiencing acute liver failure. The children, ages six and eight, died within hours of admittance. Peters soon followed. White was able to survive long enough to enter surgery and is now recovering here, at St. Vincent Hospital.

"We contacted Alphabet Apes in regards to this issue and a company representative sent this statement via e-mail." An image of the cereal box returns to the screen. The image fades into the background and is covered by text.

*Alphabet Apes and its subsidiaries send our condolences to the White family. In the face of this tragedy we ask that anyone who has purchased a box of Alphabet Apes returns the cereal to their original place of purchase. We are issuing a recall on all boxes produced after June First of last year. We are cooperating with the FDA during the investigation of our processing plants and are committed to sharing the facts of this case with the public as soon as more information is received. The safety and security of our customers is our highest priority.*

I mute the TV as Lisa and her co-workers begin to memorialize the lost family. I turn to Glen. Tears stream down his otherwise immobile face. He looks pathetic.

"That was supposed to be you." I point the remote at the screen. My rage builds when I catch a glimpse of the children playing in a home video. "You fucking killed them."

Glen tries to shake his secure head and his muffled voice wanes beneath the tape. His eyes plead with me, but it just makes me hate him even more. I get up to stand over him. For the first time since this all started, my mind is clear. I leave Glen alone long enough to return to the kitchen. I throw the drawers open until I find a knife long enough that it will do some damage.

When Glen sees me round the corner with the chef's knife, he tries to break free of the ties that hold him down. The rope digs into his skin as he drags beneath it. One of the knots loosens under the pressure of his heft. I see the rope slipping and lunge at him.

The knife sinks into him with little effort the first time, but my second pass hits bone and I have to push my body behind it to get it in. Hot blood pours out over my hands, but I don't stop. The knife slices through a band of rope and it snaps free. Glen rises out of the chair and tries to knock me down, but I slash his thigh and he falls to the floor. His legs are still hooked in the ropes around the recliner. He grabs at the carpet

332

with his hands and tries to pull himself toward the door, but the knife finds him again.

I don't know how many times the blade hits him before he stops moving. But when he does, I try to stop moving, too. I pant hard. Each inhale is ragged and full of the metallic taste of blood. Each exhale is a whoosh of relief, pushing the rage out of my exhausted body. I look down to find that I'm straddling Glen's hips. The back of his shirt is soaked in blood, and a pool of the sticky red liquid collects in the carpet around us.

There is a moment of relief when I realize that Glen is dead, but the peace is broken by a wave of fear. I look down at the knife and the blood that drips from my hands. I drop the knife onto Glen's back and get up with a start. I try to wipe the blood from my shirt, but the stains just spread across the fabric.

I take a few deep breaths and wrap my arms around my body. I must force myself to calm down so that I can figure out what to do. Glen is still, and I wish he wasn't. I wish that I could take it back. I look through watery eyes at the disarray around me and realize that the only way for me to walk away from this is clean Glen's house. They won't let me go home if they know I've been here. I rush to the kitchen, nudging cabinets open with the toe of my shoe to keep my hand prints off the wood. I look for cleaning gloves, and shouldn't be surprised when I can't find any. I notice that my shoes have tracked footprints across the linoleum and kick them off. I'm careful to stay off the red stains with my socks and cross the house to find the bathroom. Glen has a single ratty towel flung across his shower rod. I push the bathroom cabinet open with my foot and find two more. I wash my hands twice in the sink under warm water until it falls away from my skin in a clear stream and dry them on one of the clean towels. I drape the fabric over my hand and use it as a glove to open up as many cupboards and cabinets as I can find, but still can't find much more to clean with than a bar of hair-covered soap in the shower and an empty bottle of hand sanitizer on the back of the sink.

I move back to the living room and stand just outside the growing ring of blood in the carpet. I am trying to decide whether or not to go buy cleaning supplies to bring back to Glen's house when there is a knock at the front door. The rap is brief, and is quickly followed by the shadow of someone walking past the front window. I jump behind the wall that divides the living room and the entryway and in my haste to stay out of sight I bump Glen with my foot.

The sound of a large truck starting fills the house. The driver hits the gas, and before long the engine noise has faded away. I take a step back toward the door and a single red footprint appears in the carpet behind me.

"Shit." I peel the wet sock from my foot and lean to dab it in more blood. I scrub the damp fabric across the stain, disfiguring it until it is more of a blob than a footprint. I strain to reach one of the towels left in the entryway and wipe my foot with it. The blood is stubborn, so I resort to wrapping the whole towel around my foot. I'm careful to tuck the dirty side of the towel against my skin and keep the clean side out of the mess on the floor.

I move on all fours, collecting the other two towels as I go. I return to the kitchen, tie my shoe laces together and drape them over my neck. I wipe the quickly drying shoe prints with the towels. I'm not able to fully remove the blood stain from the floor, but at least succeed in disfiguring the prints. I inch my way back to the front door, doing my best to keep the floor behind me clean.

I crack the door open, using one of the towels to keep my prints off the door. The neighborhood is quiet. I push the screen door and it stops against a large box propped up on the porch. I hesitate for a minute, reading the label.

The shipping label says it's from eBay, and the return address is from an address in Hollywood. I wonder if Glen finally found a way to order his crossbow after all.

# Caught

Dougy is on the couch waiting for me when I open the door to my apartment. I stand in the doorway, trying to decide how I'm going to explain the bundle of bloodstained towels in my arms and the shoes tied around my neck.

Despite my appearance, Dougy doesn't bother to get up. "Took you long enough to get here."

"I had a few errands to run after work."

"I'm not talking about your commute from the office." Dougy's voice is flat and tired. He picks up the pocket notebook from my day in the woods with Smith from the coffee table and flips through the pages.

My feet shuffle. They want to run, but I know that with Dougy here the police aren't far away. "I needed a drive to clear my head."

"They said you drove erratically."

"It's hard to concentrate on the road when you are barefoot with your shoes tied around your neck."

Dougy sighs and slumps against my couch. He's gathered the last of the Alphabet Apes prizes around him and he rests his head on a giant stuffed caterpillar. He closes his eyes and for a minute I think he's fallen asleep. I feel nauseous when I realize how little of a threat he thinks me to be, even with all I've done. I drop the towels where I stand and walk into the kitchen to get a glass of water. The shoes get in my way at the sink, so I unwrap the laces from my neck and set them on the counter as neatly as a person can arrange blood soaked shoes joined at the laces.

"I could have helped you." The strength of Dougy's voice fills my apartment.

I finish pouring my glass of water and return to the living room. Between Dougy's broad body and the stacks of toys there isn't room for me on the couch. I sit cross legged on the floor before I take a long drink of water. "I thought you were helping me."

Dougy's eyes open and he fixes me with his stare. "I helped you to maintain contact with Ollie so that we could uncover more bodies. But the rest of this -" He gestures to the piles of gift cards and video games. "I would have helped if you had asked."

I shake my head. "You don't know what I was doing. I wasn't just giving away presents for charity."

Dougy's smile is tired. He looks like a parent who has had a long day of chasing a toddler and is now trying to put the hyperactive bastard to bed. "I've known what you were doing from the beginning."

"You have?"

Dougy holds a hand up in front of him to start counting off his fingers. "One, I had access to all of your therapy records. Two, you have been under continual surveillance since Ollie asked to work with you." Dougy looks up from his third finger at me and shakes his head. "Three, you are a terrible criminal."

I look down at my bloodstained arms and shirt. My bare feet stink with the smell of death. I nod in agreement.

"And four, Ollie kept me up to date on what you were planning every step of the way."

"Why would he do that?"

"It was a test, Henry." Dougy looks down on me with a mixture of tenderness and disappointment. "We wanted to see what you would do if your father tried to influence your decisions."

I rest my head in my hands. It weighs me down and I sink into a ball on the floor. Dougy is the closest thing I have to family aside from Dad and the regret I feel is so rancid that I can taste it on the back of my tongue. "I'm sorry I failed."

"You didn't fail, Henry." Dougy gives a soft smile as he rises from the couch. He comes toward me and covers me in a powerful embrace. "You succeeded beyond your father's wildest dreams."

"I don't understand." My words are muffled behind my hands.

Dougy pulls me up so that my face is even with his. "Your father has a plan for this terrible world we live in. You just helped to deliver the first message. I had hoped it would be someone else, but Ollie always knew it would be you."

I fall back from Dougy's embrace. I shake my head to try to clear my thoughts. "What message?"

"That gluttony will not be tolerated." Dougy's voice is gravelly as he thrusts his hand toward me in an offer to help me up. I look at his thick hand and all that it has represented. For so long I regarded Dougy's hand as one that offered protection. Sometimes it was more of a vice on a sordid partnership. I thought it was a symbol of the effort to bring justice to those that the world has lost. Only now do I see that it has been a hook, dragging me back to become a part of my father's plan to unleash pain on the world.

I look around the apartment in a panic. There is a bloodstain on the carpet behind where I sit. My shoes are still on the kitchen counter. Dougy shifts and I see the glint of the handcuffs that dangle from of his belt. I find my voice. "What's going to happen to me?"

"You'll be arrested." Dougy retracts his hand,

leans backward, and settles against the edge of my coffee table. "I will be the arresting officer. Once your case goes through, I will work it out so that you can continue to help your father uncover bodies."

"They'll let me do that?" I look down at my hands. A jumbled rush of emotion fills my head. Grief and gratefulness overwhelm me. "Even after all of this, they will let me help?"

Dougy nods. "It'll take some doing, but yes. There are more than a few people in the legal system who are sympathetic to the open cases. A couple of judges who want to make good on their promises to families before they retire."

We stare at one another for a few minutes, each at a loss for what to say next. The silence is interrupted by my cell phone. I fish it out of my pocket and wipe the damp streaks off of the screen before touching the button to answer. It's a call from the prison. *Press the star key to accept the charges.*

My dad's voice fills the line. He sounds cheerful as he greets me. "You've had a busy day today."

"I killed a man." My voice is small.

"I know. Inspector Douglas sent me a message as soon as it was done. I'll be honest son, I didn't think you had it in you. You've always been a little soft towards others." He clicks his tongue against his cheek. "Too quick to forgive."

"I didn't want to kill anybody. I was just going through the motions of the planning because..." My voice catches in my throat. I can feel the hotness of tears gathering behind my eyelids. I realize what I have let them do to me. I thought I was in control, but I never had control of anything. I can't believe that I was so stupid.

"Because?" Dad's voice is victorious. He knows exactly where this is going. Knows just what I'm about to say and is reveling in the satisfaction of hearing me say it.

"I just wanted you to love me," I squeak. The tears break free and the sob that rolls through me is a punch to the chest. I almost drop the phone and I hiccup with the effort of speaking. It is only now that I realize how alone I have been. How far I have come from the man I wanted to grow up to be. "I wanted Elsie to love me. I wanted Dougy to love me. I wanted Jeanne to love me."

"A person can only have one love, Hen. People delude themselves into thinking that they can love many things, or many people, at once. It's an illusion. A person only has the capacity to love one thing. Generally speaking, people love themselves but they play at having families and hobbies because that's what society tells them to do. Addicts and crooks are the only ones who are honest about it. Crackheads love crack. Gamblers love to gamble. They put those things above anyone and anything else in their lives. That's what love does.

"The people who you've clung to couldn't give you what you wanted because they had already found their one love. Your mother, Elsie, Jeanne, even Dougy. They don't always realize it, but the truth is that they are each devoted to me. They could never love you because they already love me."

The room feels cold. I cross my free arm across my chest and hug myself close to ward off the chill. I ball up my fist to keep my trembling hand from bouncing against me. He can't have the love that I have held for so long. I won't let him have it. "Jeanne doesn't love you," I whisper. "She's a lesbian."

"A lesbian who loves paternal trauma. Isn't that right? I am her golden goose, providing her with not only hours of interesting conversation but also providing her with a very lucrative livelihood. Why shouldn't she love me? After it comes out that she counseled my son, I imagine she will become somewhat of a celebrity. An expert on the hereditary psychology of the children of serial killers. I'll bet she'll even get to be on TV." His laughter crackles in the line. "It will be fame and glory for her until her sin consumes her."

Dad can't be right. I shake my head, defying him. There has to be someone who wanted me. "Elsie didn't love you. She just loves a good story. She loves MY story."

He snorts into the phone. "Elsie wouldn't have a story if it hadn't been for me. Sure, she tried. She sent me letters for months begging for an interview. I ignored her, of course. If I wanted to tell my story, I would have called Barbara Walters. Or Oprah. I certainly wouldn't waste my time with some wet behind the ears reporter from Forest Grove, Oregon." Dad laughs again as if he's just told the funniest joke he's ever heard.

"But you," he takes a moment to compose himself before continuing in a hushed tone, "when I finally saw her photo, I knew that you would talk to her. So I wrote her back and told her to get in touch with Inspector Douglas. The rest, as they say, is history."

"Why would Dougy help you?" I spit the

344

words out and instantly realize my mistake. Dougy gets up from the floor and stretches his back. He rolls his neck to loosen tight muscles, then unhooks the handcuffs hanging from his belt. They glint in the light and I feel the stab of his betrayal. "He's supposed to be my friend."

"He is a friend, Hen. But Inspector Douglas has dedicated the majority of his life to me. He's been tied to me longer than he's known his current wife. We've been bonded since before his children were born. He would rope the moon for me if I asked him to."

Dougy's nod indicates that he can hear every word of the conversation leaking from my cell phone. The movement is jerky but unquestioning.

Dad whispers. "I consider him to be my most devoted follower."

"And what about me?" I wipe the tears from my eyes.

"You needed to be taught a lesson, and in doing so taught a lesson to others."

"And what exactly was I supposed to learn, Dad?"

"You need to learn to forgive."

I hold the phone tight against my face while I try to find the will to speak. What right does this man have to ask anything of me? When my voice emerges, it is unsteady. "What exactly do you want me to forgive?"

Dad's voice shrinks. The cockiness of his ego fades and suddenly he is my father again. "I need you to forgive me. For killing your mother." His tone softens as the words come, and they are worn with guilt

I wipe my eyes with hands covered in the blood of another man, but in my mind the blood is my mother's. My breath escapes my chest, but it is her breath. She dies in my arms all over again. I set my jaw and growl, "I won't."

A soft cry comes from his end of the phone. He mutters about something from our past. A moment neither of us can retrieve or repair. "Can you at least understand how something can get so terribly out of control? Can you see how so many things go according to plan for weeks, months, or years without incident and then suddenly in one minute it all unravels around you? The one thing you think will never happen does, and then the world ends and you are left alone." His voice drifts into cryptic mumbles. Then he utters, "Can you at least understand that?"

I think back over our last few months together. How I pretended to plan a murder but didn't want anyone to die. How all the pieces fell into place so that I could kill without getting caught. That I was sure I could make the world a better place by removing just one person from the equation. How that one person defied me, causing harm to come to others. People who I wanted to protect. Children I had hoped would never be put in harm's way. "Yes. I do understand. But it isn't right. This isn't the way it's supposed to be."

Dad's cries fill the phone. Dougy leaps forward and takes it from me. He presses his ear against my phone and whispers tender assurances into the mouthpiece to counter Dad's sobs. Dad's voice comes out of the speaker from beneath Dougy's grip on the phone. He suddenly sounds so far away, trapped in a world that I may never be part of again. "I loved her, Hen. I loved her more than anything. I shouldn't have lost my temper. I should have given it all up and been the man she wanted me to be." His breath catches in the grief trapped within. He gasps for air. "I loved her," he wails. "I loved her and she's gone."

I lift myself from the floor. My father's tears will never be able to fill the holes in my heart or lighten the shadows cast upon my soul. But there is something in his voice that reminds me of my own sorrow. My own longing for the life we should have had.

Dougy turns his back on me as he whispers to my father. "It's all right, Ollie. Henry will learn to forgive you. Give it time. Don't worry about what's going on right now. I'm going to take care of everything."

Despite the despair that rages through my body, I am jealous of the way Dougy cradles the phone that holds my father's voice. I don't know how to join in the familiarity that Dougy and my father share, so instead I reach my hand out to meet Dougy's shoulder. His shirt is cool and smooth beneath the grime of my skin, but a feeling of comfort radiates past the bloodstains. Dougy puts his hand over mine.

There is a knock at the door and an officer enters without waiting for an answer. A second officer enters and looms behind me. "Time to go," one of them grunts.

"Goodbye, Dad." I whisper my departure even though I know Dougy has already hung up the phone. He nods toward the other officers and pulls my hand from his shoulder. He holds my hand tight as he wraps one of the cuffs around my wrist and I grip his hand in return. I squeeze it hard until a second hand rips it away, one of the other officers interpreting my gesture as noncompliance. Dougy pulls the offending wrist behind me and pairs it with the other, tightening them in the frigid handcuffs.

The officers pull me toward the door, but Dougy stays in place. I pull to a stop. "Wait, Dougy, are you going to help me?"

Dougy tilts his head. "I'm sorry, Henry but there isn't much that I can do. You killed that family. Even if you truly believe their deaths aren't you're fault, you are certainly the one who killed Glen. The evidence is everywhere."

One of the officers shifts his weight toward the door and I almost fall over. "But you promised Dad that you would take care of me."

Dougy's entire body changes. The once soft edges around his eyes are sharp again, the way they were when I was a kid. He seems bigger now than he was when he was cooing into the phone to my father. More in control. He looks at the officers and commands, "When you've got him in the car, get someone in here with some evidence boxes. Make sure they get the shoes on the counter and don't disturb the shoe treads. Swab this blood stain on the carpet. It's going to match the homicide victim in Tanasbourne."

"You said you'd help me!" My anger pushes me toward Dougy. When I reach the end of my restraints I am rewarded by being slammed back against the doorjamb by the two officers. I thrash against the bodies of the two men beside me, wild abandon taking over. I feel as though the rage could spew forever, but it isn't long before the officers have my limbs locked, their arms and legs wound around me.

Dougy strides toward me and pats me on the shoulder. When he does, I feel the weight of something slip into my shirt pocket. Dougy winks at me. "Get him out of my sight, boys."

The officers march me outside. My neighbors stand in the newly fallen rain, leaning over balcony rails and lined up on the sidewalk with curious expressions. I can feel their eyes bore into me and hear the old lady with a walker say, "It's always the quiet ones."

Dougy follows a few paces behind us and barks to get me in a car and out of contact with the neighbors. The two officers pushing me along stop at a black SUV with reinforced windows. They open the door and help me slide into the vinyl coated interior. They close the door on me without a word and head back into the crowd with their peers. I'm alone in the vehicle for the moment. Dougy leans against the hood and smiles at me knowingly.

"Henry." Dad's voice is small but clear. It leaks through the damp fabric on my chest and I realize that Dougy never hung up the phone. "Everything is going to be all right. You'll see."

"Why did you do this to me?" I look through the water droplets collecting on the window. Dougy turns an officer away from the SUV. "Why couldn't you just ask me for forgiveness with words like a normal person?"

"Would you ever have granted me that forgiveness if I would have asked?" Dad's question hangs in the air.

I think back on all of the years that I have harbored anger towards my father. Anger at his lack of restraint. The unfairness of his hobbies. The abandonment of everyone in my life because of my association with him. "No."

"I had to show you how being special feels, first. It's an incredible feeling, isn't it? Tomorrow morning, everyone will know your name. They will see your face and recognize you for the greatness that you hold inside. You are famous. The famous son of a famous man. Maybe now that you know how special you are, you can find it in yourself to forgive me."

I shake my head. The flashing police lights

351

compete with the drop in my adrenaline and make me feel woozy. "I can't. All of this is just too much. You used me. And for what? Just so I could spend the rest of my life in prison?"

Silence fills the cabin of the SUV. I look down at the pocket on the front of my shirt. The screen has turned off but the tiny green light at the top of the phone still glows bright against the fabric. Dad finally sighs. "It's all right. We will have plenty of time to work this out once your trial is over. We're going to push for you to be housed here in Sheridan. Once you're here, if you follow the rules they'll let you out in general population. I lead a Bible study that meets on Thursdays in the rec room. There are only a couple of other men who come, but they would be delighted to meet you."

"Bible study?" I am struck with the absurdity of what my father is saying. I twist my face in confusion as I look down at the phone. "Is that supposed to be some kind of consolation prize for losing everything? Why the fuck would I want to come to Bible study in prison?"

"Because, son. You are my very first disciple."

My stomach rolls when the gravity of the title sinks in. "No. I'm not a disciple of anything. I just made a mistake." The call goes silent and hot tears of regret begin to roll down my cheeks. "I've made so many mistakes."

I look up at Dougy and he holds up his hand up to mime a phone against his face. He mouths at me, "Still talking?" I shake my head at him furiously and he waves over the officer who tried to enter the vehicle earlier. The officer enters the driver's seat with a grumble, then brings the engine and the lights to life. Dougy moves to the side of the vehicle and his arm reaches toward me in a silent farewell as I am driven out of the lot.

A small blonde reporter bursts out of a van across the street and races to push a microphone into Dougy's face while a camera man trails behind to catch the shot. It isn't until he pushes the microphone from his face and turns her away that I realize the reporter is Elsie. Dougy has kept his word. Elsie may get her story, but she'll have to piece it together from across the street with everyone else.

I look down at the phone in my pocket. The light has gone out.

354

## About the Author

D.K. Greene is a self induced workaholic who writes novels and chases other fantastic dreams. After growing up in the Portland area, Greene attempted an escape to the isles of Hawaii. Following a series of sunburns and the discovery of Thalassophobia, she returned to the pacific northwest where water falls from the sky instead of rises up from the sea.

Greene creates a variety of fictional worlds under the umbrella of Kawaii Times, the publishing group that houses most of her other personalities. Other authors in her mental vault include Denise Kawaii and D.K. Rogers. You can check out D.K.'s less murderous works on http://KawaiiTimes.com.

Fans (and anti-fans) of Greene's books can contact her at Author@KawaiiTimes.com. Praise, requests for book club appearances and signings are always welcome. If you don't have anything nice to say, go ahead and say it but be aware that you may be written in as a mutilated corpse in the next book.